CRIMES AGAINST
POSTERITY

A NOVEL BY

A.R. MILLER

To those yet to be born:

You deserve better.

Introduction

Every so often, when the world seems doomed for disaster, as it has such an incorrigible habit of seeming, a revolutionary character comes along to capture the hearts and minds of the masses, rousing them to join a crusade that promises to change the course of history for the better. Defiant in the face of seemingly insurmountable obstacles and unimaginable odds, these guardians of humanity boldly call upon the snoozing human condition and ask it to snap out of its defeatist slumber and rise to whichever challenge happens to be threatening it at the time. The message has so often been, we can climb the highest mountains, traverse the stormiest seas, slay the most bulbous-nosed and wart-ridden goblins, and, to be sure, remove swords stubbornly wedged in stone in order to make things safer for children at play. These are our heroes.

Villains, on the other hand, understand that, as merchants of evil, the market for heroes must begin and end with them. In the same way that disease is required for epidemiologists to find purpose in this life, villains know that they are at the forefront of job creation and growth for heroes. Without the industriousness of villains, there is no demand for our vaunted heroes, leaving them directionless and, consequently, melancholic by way of neutering the destiny they'll never know they would have had in the first place. Without villains, the job board for heroes yields zero search results.

Rather than vilifying our villains, then, perhaps it is fairer and wouldn't hurt us all that much to show them a tincture's drop of gratitude and a teaspoon's worth—exact, not heaping—of respect. Without their insatiable drive to poison and exploit society in exchange for their own selfish gain and perverted sense of power, our steed-mounted knights become eunuchs, unable to fulfill what had been preordained at birth. In a world without villains, what good are heroes?

In recognition of their pivotal role as job creators, let us keep a healthy distance and cautiously tip our caps to villains of all stripes for bringing about the conditions required for the emergence of heroism. Whether it be an individual mastermind or a large collection of co-conspirators, without villains, it's difficult to imagine what stories, if any, would be remotely worth telling. Tales of teeth being brushed haphazardly and other such mundane and yawn-inducing things, to be sure.

The more the tales of heroes are told, the more, it seems, the lore surrounding the magnitude of their feats (and the great size of their feet) swells from a pebble's ripple in a pond to a mighty tidal wave borne from a belch in Poseidon's breast. For, exaggeration is relentless in its aspiration to humbly serve and promote the greatness of heroes, bustling about ever so eagerly to win the vaunted post of personal handmaiden. Where the stories of great heroes go, exaggeration can be found close at hand, touching up makeup, fixing an out-of-place hair or two, drafting speeches, dusting off pedestals, fielding questions, and pinching cheeks to produce that unshakably confident mythological glow.

It is in this very way that heroes cross over from the finitude of life's heartbeats to the annals of immortality, from delicate and flawed mortals to demi-gods. It is how their reputation is inflated into a thunderous bellow that echoes across the ages. Heroism requires unquestionable merit, granted, but pairing it with our loyal and outspoken sycophant is the only way to ensure its legend endures without end. No exaggeration.

But behind the iridescent myths and larger-than-life statues of every Joan of Arc, Boudica, William Wallace, Rosa Parks, Mohandas Gandhi, or Bobby Sands lies a frail and fallible creature who, in addition to leading the charge for whichever cause has resulted in their meteoric rise to fame, has been brought to their knees by the common cold; rendered paralyzed by bouts of the black dog; been infected by the parasite *insecurus sapiens*; and been pulled in all directions by a conscience that is equal parts fluid, flimsy, and faltering.

Our heroes reach the summit of Mount Olympus not because they are deities sent on a secret mission to save feeble humanity, but because they find the strength in their own feebleness to say: "I am mortal, and will die whether I shelter myself with the ambition of living as long as possible, when I have lost my teeth, hearing, and marbles, or whether I am willing to put it all on the line at any age to help make the world a better place for all or even some of its inhabitants. Should it mean death prior to the onset of dementia, so be it. I unflinchingly choose the latter."

Heroes, you see, aren't frightened by death or vulnerability; they embrace both. They accept their own inevitable end in order to summon courage in the face of adversity. To stand up for what they believe in, heroes find the conviction to confront Goliath once and for all, against all odds—the brave soul in the schoolyard who risks a bruising to stop a bully from picking on the helpless, making clear to each gobsmacked onlooker that the era of fear has come to a close. This is *our* playground. Join me, and together we can oust this tyrannical oppressor and reclaim our liberty.

Heroes are not born special. Their genes are susceptible to cancerous mutations like anyone else's (for the time being). Having their weekly allowance withheld during adolescence, the hero might very well steal from mother's purse to secure a coveted fix of chocolate from the corner store. The hero masturbates, gives off foul odours when having gone more than a day without washing, and wishes things said could be taken back. The hero didn't get the job they applied for, and, on top of that, disappointed their sexual partner, never to be given a second chance. The hero's biochemical makeup is, on the whole, indistinguishable from the disgruntled and unhappy commuters crowding them on the train. The hero is as pathetic and worthy of sympathy as they are exceptional and worthy of praise; an ordinary life filled with extraordinary potential.

The hero is *you*.

Prologue

Death. The greatest mystery of life doesn't reveal itself until the end, thereby remaining cloaked from all those who've yet to see beyond its grim curtain. Once that curtain has been drawn, well, that's where this sentence ends.

The unthinkably frightening prospect of life ending in absolute nothingness has the power to compel much of the world's population to believe—with such zeal they shut themselves off completely from any considerations to the contrary—in that which ultimately cannot be proven. These are the meek, humble servants and worshippers of a higher power. Those among us who believe devoutly that they will live on for eternity so long as they carry out *His* will to the letter and beg for forgiveness whenever, as a result of incurable flaws and weaknesses, they transgress. They hold sacred their beliefs without requiring any scientific evidence that their God really exists, save for a few miraculous anecdotes that date back thousands of years. To them, that is faith. Such is the leap one must take. For who are we mere mortals to call into question the omniscience of the creator and overseer of *everything*? *He* is carrying out *His* plan in accordance with *His* word and judging our performances with *His* all-seeing eye in the process, as if existence itself were one continuously running test to satisfy *Him*. Failure to do so will result in a sentence of consecutive eons tiptoeing along an endless terrain of scorching fire and brimstone. Sounds like hell, right? Question *Him* if you dare.

But many do dare. A large and growing segment, in fact. These are the atheists among us, the existential risk-takers who laugh brazenly in the face of religious dogma. They are the ones who claim to be too intellectual, too cerebral, too temporal, too empirical to get swept up in all the hocus-pocus. To them, religion is nothing more than fiction and superstition, an archaic form of social control necessary to sustain an established order and keep the poor, helpless, and, for related reasons, sickly masses in shackles, cowering at the deeply ingrained threat of God's needy and narcissistic wrath. It's all too obvious, they'll state; when all is said and done, human life will have been nothing more than an evolutionary blip in an impossibly vast cosmos that feels neither this way nor that about us. Any broader significance that humans attribute to their existence is a delusional means of finding relevance in an irrelevant life. Human-centric meaning-making at its best.

The reality, the atheists claim to know better, is that, after a number of years spent collecting food and drink to fuel us to grow and reproduce, the voice in our head—our sentience—will be extinguished for good like the flick of a switch cutting off electricity from a light bulb. From there, our bodies rot, reintegrating into and enriching the soil in order that a forget-me-not, for example, may grow. How fitting. That is the closest we will ever come to achieving immortality. Through the natural cycle of life's seasons, our disintegrated particulate forms reintegrate with other matter to take on new shapes, sizes, and species. Live life to the fullest, they will say, for you will one day run out of tomorrows and that will be it.

Like their religious counterparts, non-believers are, of course, convinced that their worldview is the correct one (the confirmation bias is strong in each of us). Rather than stemming from a need to believe in the promise of immortality, the atheist's arrogance stems from a conviction that they are smarter, more fearless, and more open-minded than the flocks of sheep who blindly and gullibly drink grape juice on Sundays, remove their shoes to enter a temple, or trek to Mecca to press their foreheads against the arid soil beneath them. Religion is the cause of all the world's ills, they might antagonistically profess, while they go on living life according to their will, not *His*. It's as if they take pride in crushing what they view as the naïve and false hope of others.

In response, the pious will pray for the lost and corrupted souls of these heretics in an attempt at saving them from damnation. And perhaps their prayers do get answered from time to time, for the closer those who reject God come to their final breath, the shakier the foundation supporting their opposition to *Him* seems to become. How often have we heard stories of longstanding atheists having eleventh-hour changes of heart on their deathbeds and making last-gasp conversions to religion, as if quite literally tossing up a Hail Mary to redeem themselves at their life's final buzzer? Legend has it that the father of evolution himself, one Charles Darwin, had second thoughts just moments prior to departing this world. Amazingly, this account was first spoken from the lips of one Lady Hope, who was at the great scientist's bedside during his final hours. Perhaps the Lord works in mysterious ways, after all. Perhaps humans are highly skilled at weaving convincing tales. Perhaps both. Who knows?

Finally, there are the agnostics, the Goldilockses of faith. These are the moderates among us, who don't have a religion, per se, but who claim there is an underlying force that permeates and connects all things. Their spirituality is rooted in a belief in universal energy. For them, there is neither an all-powerful creator nor grounds for nihilism. Instead, they believe everything is made up of an essential force that is at once palpable and undetectable. When we die, we neither go off to a make-believe heaven nor perish forever into nothingness; the energy contained within the confines of our flesh-and-bone temples is merely released back into the universe to resume its eternal dance, vibrating along astral planes at the outer limits of the cosmos. There is nothing to be afraid of. We are all of us and forever inextricably linked through this foundational power grid. The light in me honours the light in you, they say. *Namaste.*

The benefit of adopting an agnostic belief system, of course, is that one foot can remain on the sand while the other is submerged in the sea. By playing both sides, this camp has effectively hedged its bets between this life and the next. If death is the end, and emptiness, less than blackness even, is what awaits us, these generalist believers have had the opportunity to enjoy all the earthly pleasures without fear of reprisal, thanks to their carefully balanced fence-sitting. If their spiritual hypothesis is correct, they'll dissipate into their essential energetic form and join the great quantum tango as pulsating particles. If, on the other hand, the Divine Comedy turns out to be no laughing matter, and they are subjected to a final judgment by an omnipotent God to determine whether they are to be cast off into the Inferno or granted passage into Heaven, they'll likely receive marks for their loose commitment to spirituality and be issued a conditional pass beyond the pearly gates. Did you get an A+ in divinity class? No, but I passed and still got to enjoy Heaven's bounty.

But back to death. Belief system notwithstanding, everyone dies. Period. In the same way the lack of consensus regarding how the universe came into being doesn't conflict with unanimous agreement over the fact that it *did*, we can all agree that the grim reaper awaits us, even if we're at odds over what follows. What is it? What happens to the narrative voice inside our head when we go? Any person claiming to know the answer to this age-old question is simply postulating about what occurs posthumously. Dead men tell no tales. Skeletons remain in their coffin-shaped closets. The truly honest and self-aware among us will summon the nerve to accept the unknown for precisely what it is—the unknown.

And while we would be deluding ourselves by claiming to know what awaits us when we expire, we have a fairly good idea of what to expect the instant before. This phenomenon has been reported by countless unrelated adults and children across the ages who have had near-death experiences despite being declared clinically dead by the scientific standards of their times. Adults and children who have stood at death's massive door, rapped on its ghoulish knocker, and been turned away by a cadaverous butler. In each of these cases, separated by time, space, and cultural influences, people have reported the same paranormal happening: in the infinitesimal interval that acts as the definitive threshold between life and death, their lives have flashed before their eyes. It is as if, during our penultimate moment, before that fabled bright light comes into view, the story of our life is replayed in the mind's eye at warp speed, a concluding curtain call before we vanish into the mystical unknown.

And this is where the journey of our story's protagonist begins, at its end. With blood pouring out of him, his life flashed before his eyes.

I

All that was remarkable about the mobile home was that it was unremarkable. Replete with emptiness save for various stains, cigarette burns, and a tower of sauce-smeared disposable plates, it was an image devoid of love, and it filled the heart with sadness.

A lone couch sat in the middle, its transparent plastic covering so cracked and fogged that the hideous floral-patterned material it had initially been intended to preserve was barely discernible. Through squinting eyes, the couch might have resembled the last, great sub-Saharan land mammal after having collapsed under its own weight in conditions too inhospitable to bear. Elephant or rhinoceros, it mattered not; it was unable to go on, and, consequently, neither was the species whose fate it carried on its wearied back.

In front of the couch stood a sickly-looking TV dinner tray, on top of which rested a mostly polished off bottle of the cheapest spirit the underground pain killer trade could buy. A malnourished flamingo bred for servitude, the weight under which the tray's knock knees trembled had been lessened by degrees with each maniacal swig taken from the bottle it held up, transferring the wobbling legs from the tray to an awakening monster who had so graciously reduced the tray's load.

While Jekyll morphed into Hyde in the background, a young boy played with mismatched toys on the frayed carpet. Shielded from his toxic surroundings by the force field of his own imagination, the boy was only vaguely aware of the rising tension brewing mere feet away. More concerned was he with the naked doll who had set out on a great adventure on a miniature toy car to rescue their friend, the spinny thing from the evil empty glass-cleaner bottle.

Outmatched by the enormity of their adversary, the inanimate duo had to put their head and engine together and quickly decide upon a strategy. The clock was ticking (ironically, the cheap clock dangling on the wall had stopped working long ago). After a short huddle, a plan of attack was established. As the uninhibited doll tossed rocks—stale crumbs that littered the carpet—to create a diversion, the car quite literally floored it, stubbing the vile spray container's toe with such force that it successfully felled and slayed the menacing giant once and for all. *Timber,* the boy thought as he relished his earliest notion of good triumphing over evil.

In almost the same instant as the plastic ogre came crashing to the floor, a much more violent and loud crash took place in the room, snapping our satisfied orchestrator of happy endings out of the safety and comfort of his fantasy world and returning his attention to the cruel reality into which he had been unfairly born. As his developing mind worked to quickly piece together the connection between the fragments of glass littering the ground and the fact that the bottle that once stood atop the TV tray was no longer anywhere to be found, he intuited that it had either been thrown by or had flown away in fear of the angry man whose only purpose seemed to be tormenting him and his poor mother.

Not only was his mother poor, but she was also helpless, making her an easy target for someone who dealt with unresolved emotional pain by unleashing it on others. And that he did, striking her repeatedly with his remorseless fist. It seemed he was in an especially vicious and unforgiving mood on this occasion.

Mostly out of an effort to drown out the unbearable sound of his mother's screams, the boy let out a colicky wail, his lungs a resounding bagpipe played by a strapping Scotsman. These piercing cries drew the ire of the gutless attacker, reminding him that he had unceremoniously left his other helpless victim unattended. Blind to the fact that he himself had caused the incessant howling that infuriated him, the abuser-in-chief left the defenseless and now whimpering woman in a heap of her own blood and tears and made his way over to the boy in large, lumbering steps that seemed to pound out, *Fee fi fo fum, I smell the blood of someone else who can't possibly defend himself.*

Picking up a tattered and stained pillow with which he planned on suffocating the boy to death just to shut him up, the weak-minded man, in his ongoing bid to convince himself that he was in total control of every situation, towered over the helpless child, casting a storm cloud's shadow under which the boy, as if suddenly encircled by an entourage of guardian angels, was swept over by an inexplicable wave of complete calm, the seas of his emotions switching from tempest to a sheet of glass in a decisive snap of Neptune's fingers.

His fragile ego now injured by the harmless child's sudden air of stoicism, the man had a change of heart. Dropping the pillow to the floor, he made a teetering about-face and collected his ill-fitting jacket from the rusty hooks jutting out from the wall. Jacket in hand, the monster leaned over the gnarled woman, as if to curtsy after what he felt was a most impressive display of domestic abuse. Pausing for effect, he allowed a viscous stream of phlegm-infused saliva to bungee from his chapped lips onto her grimacing face. With a confluence of tears, blood, and lung sewage dripping from her cheek, the woman winced a blend of agony and disgust. The monster then straightened up to his characteristic hunched posture and departed the downtrodden residence with a limp and a gleam of satisfaction in his eye. The door slammed behind him. *Exeunt demon.*

Our boy sat in complete stillness, his young life already plagued by tragedy. Through no choice or fault of his own, circumstance had corrupted the innocence of his upbringing. He was destined for a stunted emotional development and troubled future right out of the gate. Thus, his earliest understanding of happiness wasn't the presence of joy, but rather the absence of suffering. The moment after the door closed, he felt safe again; that was as good as it got. The threat was gone for the time being. Although his mother lay hemorrhaging just feet away, the worst of it was over.

Between the whimpers and moans of the woman could be heard departing footsteps outside. The crunching of gravel grew more and more distant until it eventually stopped and was followed by the piercing creak of an opening truck door. If one were to comb the entire planet, they'd be hard pressed to find a rustier vehicle still in use. Like the way that dogs have an uncanny tendency of resembling their human companions, cars and trucks can often tell us a lot about their drivers. This case was no exception: rotten from the inside out.

Somewhere deep within her physical agony and mental disorientation, our boy's mother clung on to the cliff's edge of consciousness. Her resilience, her will to go on, was rooted in her filial duty to her first and only born. With this flicker of life still burning inside, she listened carefully to her assailant's retreat. He had reached his car and opened the door. All that remained was for him to close it, turn on the engine, and go. *Just go.* Then, at least, she would know her boy was safe.

Upon hearing the closing of the truck door, she called on what little strength she had left and began to slither for the phone that lay no more than a dozen feet away. She wasn't ready to die. She had to alert the authorities. Gurgling and choking on her own blood as she crept, she listened carefully for the sound of the engine to start and for the drunkest of drivers to peel away. But the noise she so desperately hoped to hear never came.

Instead, as if God had been in a wicked mood and hit rewind on the audio recording of their lives, she again found herself listening to the sounds of lumbering footsteps on their gravel lawn, only this time they were growing louder, getting closer, sounding more determined. The monster was returning. Crunch. Crunch. Crunch.

It was a race against time. Inching along like a human slug, the boy's mother, aware that the final grains were emptying from her hourglass, redoubled her determination to reach her phone. She could barely breathe, let alone speak, so voice recognition was not an option. She would have to physically press the buttons for emergency services and hit send. As the sound of the doorknob turning reached her ears, she made a final lunge toward the phone, but her pathetic attempt amounted to little more than a convulsive gasp.

Whereas our boy's mother had for a long time been made to *feel* powerless under the constant application of physical and emotional abuse, she now understood with full force what it actually meant to *be* powerless. Prone and incapable of protecting her young, she was livestock helplessly observing the final approach of a butcher. Her son would be at his mercy. It was double torture.

Thankfully, her impending death would be at the hands of a most humane killer. One who, rather than draw out her suffering with more of his boring, predictable use of blunt force, had returned from his truck with a loaded shotgun in hand. With the gun's double barrel pointing at her blood-matted skull from close range, she heard the innocent voice of her baby boy call to her. He spoke in the same way he might on one of those peaceful Saturday mornings, the rare cherished time of the week when they could forget all their worries and spend serene hours together at the public park.

In a last-ditch attempt to protect her child from sharing her untimely fate, she drew a deep breath with which to plead with her assailant to spare her son's life. Tragically, she inhaled blood along with air, like a vacuum sucking up spilt tomato juice. This, of course, caused her to choke, and the abruptness of the noise startled the gunman, causing his already trembling trigger finger (a condition brought about by years of substance abuse, not nerves associated with the severity of the situation) to fire at its intended target prematurely. Bang.

If it's true that the emotional fallout of the years before the age of five lasts the rest of a human's life, witnessing the brutal murder of one's own mother during such an impressionable stage of physical and mental development must surely leave an indelible emotional scar that, like a physical scar on a young child's elastic skin, will only stretch and become more pronounced with age. And yet, at that moment, after the deafening gun blast that left his mother's skull a smashed melon strewing entrails across the remains of a once delicate and beautiful face, there was a serenity and composure about our boy, as if he, at such a tender age, had the wisdom to tame fear in the face of grave danger.

After taking a few moments to admire his gruesome accomplishment, our orchestrator of death slowly turned his gaze to the boy and grinned the singularly malevolent grin of one who wishes to convey—*you're next.*

Sauntering across the room with the confident air of someone who has nary a care in the world, the boogeyman waved the gun gracefully through the air, as if conducting a requiem for the deaf. Kneeling before the boy, the remorseless monster ran his thumb gently down the soft contours of the child's plump face and off the cleft of his chin in a mimicry of kindness and affection. While his one hand stroked the boy's plump, young cheek, leaving streaks of crimson in its wake, his other hand reached for shells in his pockets with which to reload his firearm. How fortunate are those children who will only ever be exposed to *seashells by the seashore?*

Temporarily deafened by the blast that left his mother lifeless, our boy could not hear a word of the twisted and convoluted last rites being slurred in his direction. He could, however, feel the pressure of a cold kiss of death being imprinted onto one rosy cheek by the steel lips of the shotgun's twin barrel opening. Through it all, our boy remained astonishingly composed.

Able to hear nothing more than a high-pitched ringing, our boy was also deaf to the growing sound of approaching police sirens. The monster standing above him knew very well what the sounds meant. And so, in a betrayal of the true cowardice that lay beneath the surface of all passion-driven killers, the man decided that more gunfire would only serve to draw unwanted attention to the specifics of his location, leading to his certain capture. He eased his finger from the trigger, lowered the gun, and decided he'd be better off fleeing both the scene and the responsibility for his abominable actions.

To rationalize his retreat to himself as anything other than spineless, the now panic-stricken monster explained to our boy that death would be letting him off too easy. He would instead condemn him to a tortured life throughout which his happiness would be held captive by the inner demons of psychological torment, where it would remain shackled to a bunk in the darkest recesses of his soul, never again to see the light of day. Content that he had produced what was tantamount to the effect of a second successful kill, the now fugitive man summoned the expertise he had acquired during his delinquent adolescence and slid out a side window into an intricate network of junk-filled yards. The monster's fate would forever remain a mystery to his young victim, but his haunting memory would poison him always.

Alone again were mother and son. Getting to his feet in a manner similar to a calf that had not yet mastered walking, our boy made his way over to his mother's mangled corpse. Reaching her side, the boy knelt before her as would a knight honouring his queen. After pausing momentarily to stare lovingly at the woman who had brought him into the world, he curled up alongside her in the fetal position, superimposing a return to the womb. When the police arrived, they discovered a nativity scene gone wrong. God and reason were nowhere to be found.

II

As a rule, kids complain about having to attend school. The painfully early mornings, the unthinkable amount of time spent bound to a desk, the militant lining up and waiting in silence, the insult to injury that is homework, and the many other constraints that get in the way of living every day covered in mud, with scraped knees peering out of torn blue jeans, as if life itself were *Lord of the Flies*—which, ironically, would mean never having to read it. Immersion into this early world of unnatural structure and discipline has produced countless acts of rebellion, including feigned illnesses, incomplete homework assignments, and the greatest intellectual affront of all—plagiarism.

But once the drudgery of academia has been peeled away, school is, overall, a wonderful staple of childhood and adolescence for most students. School is where we meet, make, and spend a larger bulk of time with friends than any other time in life; because classmates are, by and large, far more likable and tolerable than co-workers.

School is where many learn and fail at romance for the first time. It is where we fine-tune (or fall flat trying) our comedic selves. It is where we discover our hidden talents and take up lifelong pursuits. It is where we first develop outside the family unit as team members and leaders. It is where we are taught far more important life lessons than any curriculum could ever lay claim to. It is where we get to experience what it means to belong to something bigger. School is where our dreams seem most realistic and attainable, as they've not yet been put to the test in the real world, where they so often are crushed.

Of course, these generalities do not describe everyone's school experience. For children who spend their early scholastic years friendless or fearful of bullies, each day is a waking nightmare. Each bodily bruise, each mental scar is another setback to their chance at a healthy social development. The harder they try, the worse it gets. Acceptance and happiness are shadows not worth chasing. Their right to a safe and meaningful student experience is replaced by such incredibly deep and troubling emotional pain that many will never bounce back as long as they live.

After having bounced around the foster care system following the murder of his mother, our traumatized boy finally landed a stable living situation in a towering Victorian home owned by a wealthy elderly couple. Having sworn off children after a cursed string of miscarriages earlier in life, the couple had recently decided to adopt a would-be heir to their fortune as a legacy that would extend beyond the inevitability of the grave, an impending reality that had become increasingly apparent each time they examined the wrinkled, sallow, and greying faces staring at them from the mirror.

With no shortage of love, attention, and resources now available to him, the living situation our damaged boy found himself in had all the trappings of a privileged life. To say that opportunity was suddenly at his disposal would be an understatement of gigantic proportions.

But home is to the orphan as legs are to the paraplegic: foster family as prosthesis. For our oft-displaced little boy, emotional scarring teamed up with abandonment issues to engrain in him extreme suspicion and resentment toward even the most well-intentioned folk. Utterly lacking in self-worth, our boy was unable to trust anything about the world around him. Like a flower that has been transplanted over and over again, winding up in a lavish botanical garden was not enough to put his damaged roots at ease. Stability was perceived as nothing more than a mirage. Love was a trick being played by the devil, who followed him in disguise everywhere he went. Shielding himself from further suffering was our boy's overriding objective. The imagined protective shell in which he encapsulated himself was his sole means of feeling a sense of control over the cruel world around him.

To make matters worse, the private elementary school he attended—the finest in the land—failed to provide our jaded young soul with a safe space. While the small class sizes and high-caliber faculty afforded by steep tuition fees produced in him a strong scholarly foundation, he would always be a social outsider with no way in. He was different. He knew it and his peers knew it. It was accepted among the student body that he was not accepted among the student body. Not one of his classmates ever invited him to collaborate on group projects. No one sat and ate with him at lunch. No one played with him during recess. When he walked the halls, the sense of alienation and disparagement was palpable. Not a word had to be spoken in order to observe the process of social ostracization in action. The sidelong glances and snickers. The pronounced throat clears to interrupt mindless gossip and signal the approach of an outsider—a *loser*. The intentional jostles to cause him to bump into others as if he were a human pinball, enrolled in that school only for the amusement of others. The pretty girls straining to contain their laughter, but doing so overtly in hopes of being noticed by the cool boys. And, of course, the stray leg thrust into his path, causing our poor (but now rich) boy to fall headlong into the feet of one of the only girls in the entire school (read: entire world) who had ever been remotely nice to him. In this situation, however, with a jury of her peers gauging her reaction, the social pressure was too unbearable to react in a way that was natural to her and felt right. Rather than doing the decent thing and helping him up, she went against her better judgment and resisted her own humanity, instead sidestepping our boy's pathetically sprawled-out body with a look of disgust on her face. Naturally, her reaction was met with laughter and approval.

Thus was the daily experience of our boy during his time at elementary school. There was only a single door he knew would always be open to him—the door to the classroom. It was through this threshold he forged a special bond with a most dedicated and inspirational teacher. Filled with sympathy and empathy at having learned the details of our boy's tragic story, this teacher donated of her own spare time outside regular classroom hours to provide our boy with one-to-one tutoring and, most powerfully of all, someone who genuinely cared about and listened to him—a mentor and role model.

This was no ordinary teacher, you see. She did not choose to become an educator to get summers off and end her workdays early; she did so to make a make a positive difference in the impressionable lives of children. Teaching was her way of having a lasting influence on the future. She felt a powerful calling to make the world a better place, a calling she answered daily.

She was the earliest to arrive and the last to leave each morning and afternoon. With an insatiable thirst for professional development, she took on as many continuing education courses as she could reasonably handle. As a teacher, she could never be good enough. Human potential, she believed, was limitless. Her lesson plans were no less well thought out than they were innovative and effective. She brought curricula to life and captured the hearts and minds of otherwise lackluster students. Whether it was engaging children in dramatic reenactments of salient historical events or writing sing-along songs to make the painstaking process of memorization and rote learning seem less laborious, this woman's meter stick was a magic wand that, with the elegance of a fairy queen, she used to turn the slog of primary school into an effortless joy.

During a stretch of days marked by dangerously poor air quality and unpredictably extreme weather patterns, the socially advantaged students at our boy's elite academy were some of the least impacted in all of society. Whereas the majority of school-aged kids were confined to drab classrooms, cafeterias, and gymnasiums during recesses and lunch hours each time Mother Nature sank into one of her increasingly frequent bouts of prolonged inhospitality, the lucky genetic material that attended the same prestigious campus as our boy were shuttled through an air-conditioned tunnel into their very own biodome, paid for out-of-pocket by parents in the gated community where the school was located. These children of means were literally and figuratively protected by a bubble from the mounting climatic threats affecting the world around them. Although relatively small compared with their sprawling outdoor schoolyard, students could still get a bit of exercise and social time in a temperature-controlled green space, allowing them to burn through their excesses of youthful energy. The red-faced youth could then return with calm spirits and attentive minds to their bastions of enriched learning, characterized by the three Rs as they pertain to the wealthy: resources, resources, and resources.

As one might expect, based on firsthand experiences of how nasty children can be, the campus biodome failed to shelter our boy from the inhospitable climate of bullying. Wherever his peers manifested, so, too, did his fears. Even as he roamed alone, stroking the leaves of exotic flora and minding his own business, a pack of bullies might track him down and shove him into a thorny collection of cacti (pricks!). This, of course, begged the age-old question: don't bullies have anything better to do?

Catching wind of this reprehensible behaviour through the school's grapevine, the exceptional teacher our boy so adored felt a duty to intervene. Rather than reprimand the culprits and magnify their disdain for their victim, she removed our boy from harm's way by extending an offer to join her at lunchtime and listen to her read from one of her favourite-ever books. *The Prince and the Pauper*, a classic novel, was written by Mark Twain, a famous author who had died a long time ago, but who, the teacher claimed, would live forever through his writing.

Happy just to be thought of in kindly terms and invited to take part in a fun activity with someone he not only trusted but also idolized, our boy couldn't accept the offer fast enough. Little did he know at the time, there was more to this offer than met the eye.

Behind the scenes, the dedicated teacher was conspiring with the school's headmaster on a plan to make the school a safer, more inclusive space for our boy. By knowing one of their students was the victim of chronic bullying on their watch, they had a clear obligation to act. When responsible for the children of some of the most powerful members of society, however, a school's administration can be rendered powerless in its efforts to work with parents to address the inappropriate behaviour or academic shortcomings of said parents' progeny. Any such outreach is usually met with great offence, for who would dare slight the genetic extensions of the great and mighty? Rather than assume responsibility for their children's misdeeds or poor performances, and use the school's feedback as grounds for a good old-fashioned life lesson, most parents such as these will, at best, gaslight faculty into accepting that the issue must be their fault for being incompetent—some parents will even threaten the school with legal action for slander and such. As a result, finding long-term solutions to keeping overindulged kids with malicious intentions at bay is tricky, to say the least. When annual tuition fees dwarf teachers' annual salaries, detentions, suspensions, and expulsions are difficult to broach, even in such reprehensibly extreme circumstances.

Because this extraordinary teacher was universally adored by staff and students alike, she and the principal decided she would act as a covert emissary to help convert our boy's schoolyard adversaries into his friends—bullies into allies. If they could create a safe environment for controlled integration and disguise it as an exclusive, merit-based opportunity for a chosen few standout students, they could facilitate the development of a better relationship between our boy and a handpicked selection of kids with the popularity and playground clout required to improve his social standing. If it worked, the coolest kids and highest performers in and around our boy's age would, through increased familiarity and the endorsement of the teacher, gradually come to accept him into their circle. When the impressionable herd of followers saw that our boy was accepted into the popular crowd, they would have no choice but to sheepishly follow suit. There was no harm in trying, their thinking went. Things couldn't get worse.

It was formally announced to the student body that, as a reward for their stellar achievement on a number of key measures of student success, a group of very deserving students, our boy included, would be invited to take part in a special storytelling series hosted by the school's most popular teacher for the next few weeks during lunch hours.

Shockingly (for the headmaster who privately had very little confidence in the plan from the outset), each child not only accepted their invitation with zeal, but began to strut around the school with chins held slightly higher than normal to ensure their newly acquired distinction went unnoticed by none, for they—an all too common theme in many of their young, privileged lives—were the chosen ones.

Upon learning he was not the only student who had been invited to be read to, our fragile boy became anxious and distressed. Feeling betrayed and vulnerable, as if he had been exposed to danger masquerading as safety, our boy, in a state of unbridled agitation, sought out his favourite teacher to express, in kid's terms, his disapproval with what he felt to be a duplicitous stunt. He implored her to understand that he needed protection from his peers, not more time in the lion's den. Surely she, of all people, could understand.

Compassionate as always, the saintly teacher quickly assuaged our boy's fears by explaining that she would always protect him. This was a chance for the others to get to know him and come to understand how fantastic he really was. She would make sure of it. She promised. For her, our boy was Arthur of Camelot, about to remove the sword from the stone and discover he was a king! The other kids would be there to witness his hidden powers emerge like sunbeams bursting through clouds. He just had to believe in himself the same way she believed in him. He had her word that he was safe, and her word was as good as gold. With the pep talk out of the way, she mussed the boy's hair with her hand and sent him skipping down the corridor on his merry way. His life was about to change for the better. She could feel it.

On the first day of the exclusive invitational reading series, the students were mesmerized by what awaited them beyond the classroom door. Managing to outdo herself, the teacher had transformed the classroom into an enchanted medieval world full of red tapestries, artificial animal furs and horns, brass rubbings, chainmail, helmets, swords, shields, and the like.

Guided by the spellbinding dance of candlelight, the wide-eyed children crossed over into a magical realm from the distant past. Not a word between them was spoken as they crept along with jaws wide open, observing the many artifacts and relics that transported them across time and space. After having made their way to the designated reading area, their attention suddenly shifted to the teacher, who, wearing an exquisitely detailed gown from yesteryear, was backlit by a towering wall of candles that emitted the halo everyone had always attributed to her but had never before seen with their own two eyes. Entranced to such an extent that they failed to notice the cornucopia of healthy and not-so-healthy snacks scattered about them, the children, without any verbal instruction, silently sat down as a group, as if choreographed, demonstrating to their narrator that she had their undivided attention. In an entertaining but not terribly convincing accent, she introduced the book and opened it to the first page, signifying that they were disembarking from reality and setting sail for a new and yet to be discovered world in their collective imagination.

As the story began to unfold, the carpet upon which the students sat took flight. So vivid and captivating was their experience that, after the first day's reading, it was all any of them could think about. The time between storytelling sessions was, from the perspective of their developing minds, the single greatest torture imaginable, producing that unique brand of childhood suffering grown-ups impatiently refer to as *impatience*. Each night over the course of those days and weeks carried with it an uncontainable excitement and anticipation that was tantamount to Christmas Eve. How astonishing and welcome it was for the parents and, in some cases, nannies to discover that their children had suddenly become eager for bedtime on school nights. Come morning, alarms were no longer necessary. Weekends, previously the most enjoyable days of the week, became practically unendurable.

As for the plan, it was, by all appearances, working to the letter (and sentence, and paragraph, and chapter, and so on). Together, these kids were forging a closely knit bond based on a shared experience that only they understood, for it was only they who got to experience it, as if they were the world's only members of an ultra-elite club, which, when put that way, they kind of were. With their sense of awe and wonder kindled, their budding minds were sent soaring on an enchanted voyage they were taking together. The newfound bond between each of them was made evident every time they acknowledged one another in the halls with the subtlest of head nods accompanied by irrepressible grins and the occasional giggle. They had been chosen to be part of a special club that no one else could experience or understand. These were days characterized by tremendous happiness and excitement.

For the isolated and invisible individual, to be favourably acknowledged and, taking it a giant step further, accepted by someone of a high social standing, can be an overwhelming experience. Take a homeless person or someone with a disability, for example. Accustomed to being ridiculed, pitied or, at best, ignored their entire lives, being unexpectedly treated like an everyday person rather than a freakshow exhibit can result in emotional reactions ranging from deep-seated suspicion to unbridled elation. For people such as this, getting the rare opportunity to take part in the day-to-day human experiences, interactions, and relationships most of us take for granted can feel like winning the lottery, a reality that is no less sad than true—than changeable.

For our bullied young friend, the case was no different. As he gradually came to feel more included in a group of his peers— the crème de la crème of the school—he felt, somewhere deep from within himself, that he was, at long last, being unshackled from the hardship he had been dragging around his entire life. Dismounting the carousel in his mind upon which he had spent so much time circling around his wounded past, he began to look forward with renewed hope and optimism, and—my oh my!—did it feel good.

Sitting amongst his new acquaintances each noon hour (it would be rather presumptuous and bold to label them as anything more so prematurely, as tempting as it was for him to invoke the "f" word)—sitting there with the same kids he not long ago viewed as untouchable social deities, our boy couldn't help but project his own present-day world onto the timeless tale being read. He was the social pauper who, somehow, in what felt like a most unexpected and welcome twist of fate, had found himself rubbing shoulders with royalty. He had, through an act of divine happenstance, been elevated to the status of social prince. Perhaps the teacher was right, he couldn't help but fantasize, and he was destined to one day become a king!

Belonging, to our boy, meant the world. He was a *somebody* for the first time since the passing of his mother. After school, when he was dropped off by a private valet at home, he would cut loose the dead weight that was his schoolbag on the vast and intricately manicured front lawn where he resided, and race inside as fast as his young legs would carry him to tell his foster parents, in excruciatingly fine detail, all about the day's events. And while his foster parents no longer possessed the energy stores to respond as exuberantly as he would have liked, it was all the same to him. The audience was irrelevant. What truly mattered was that he could hear himself as he spoke the words. He had finally acquired the single most important determinant of happiness in this life: friends (it had to be said!).

On the day when they were set to finish the final pages of the story, the smog that had blanketed the region for the past few weeks finally dissipated and the air became more breathable and, therefore, less damaging to the delicate lungs of children. As content as the students at the academy always were to traipse among the flora inside the school's private biodome, this bout of inhospitable conditions had been the harshest and most protracted on record. As time went on, the confines of the dome began to feel more and more limiting to the kids' abilities to fully express themselves through play. Indoor recess, even inside a private biodome, will always fall short of the real outdoors. So when it was announced that recess would resume outside on the surface of the great biosphere, the student body brimmed with excitement and anticipation like a group of young thoroughbreds waiting for the gates to the racetrack to be raised. Forgetting, for once, about the fact that they were the sons and daughters of the ultra-wealthy, the prospect of finally getting back outside for sports, games, and other tomfoolery reminded these kids that they were just that—kids. Rambunctious boys and girls who yearned to rollick in the open air, and the rosier their cheeks, the more scuffed their shoes and grass-stained their clothes, the better.

For the children taking part in the reading club, their reaction to learning that outside recess had again become an option was no different. As eager as they were to find out how their cherished story would unfold, as proud as they were of having been handpicked for the exclusive experience, there was something about the lure of being outside that awakened within them an almost animal urge—humans are animals, after all—to roam freely across the open plains, or, in this case, open football fields, baseball diamonds, basketball courts, and chalk-drawn hopscotch patterns.

That some students would spend their time outdoors playing simulated games on hand-held electronic devices while others played the real thing didn't alter the core importance of standing beneath a blue sky dotted with the occasional cotton ball cloud. What mattered, whether they were conscious of it or not, was that they were back with Mother Nature, connected, even if indirectly, to their evolutionary roots, the surest way to experience fulfillment as a species living off the very earth from which it had originated so inconceivably long ago. These children were the next generation of the planet's stewards. Whether they would one day take up the solemn duty to act as custodians for the preservation of life or flout it in the name of shortsightedness and greed remained to be seen. For now, they were kids, and, no different from the offspring of hunters and gatherers before them, they longed for one thing and one thing only—play.

That same day, as our boy approached the classroom where the exclusive reading club was held, he was, as had become the custom, greeted by the standout teacher and expert narrator he so idolized. On this day, however, he was quick to notice that she wasn't dressed in one of the elaborate costumes he had come to expect to find her wearing to greet them at the start of each lunch hour. He slowed from an excited jog to a cautious walk. What had changed? Was something wrong?

Plain clothed and smiling, she crouched down before him and asked him in a tone no less friendly than rhetorical what he was doing there. When he responded with a look of utter bewilderment, the teacher, in her kind and disarming manner, spelled out her meaning by reminding him that the air outside had cleared and that he was to join his new friends on the playground without delay.

Whereas news that they would again be able to run free in the playground brought irrepressible glee to the hearts of most of his classmates, the boy at the centre of our story found it terribly disheartening. He didn't want to go outside. He wanted to be there, with the standout teacher, in a safe setting where he finally felt he belonged. Just when he had begun to hit what for him was his social stride, the reading rug was being pulled out from under him. The person he trusted most was turning him away from the one place that made him feel included, and reintroducing him to an environment he associated with terror.

Quickly recognizing the boy's disappointment, the teacher intervened with reassuring words, that time-tested oral balm used to sooth flare-ups of inner disquiet. She explained to him that the reading group was only being temporarily put on hold so that he and his classmates could get some much-needed fresh air. That was what bookmarks were for! She went on to describe how exercise and nature were vital components of a healthy imagination, and that if he dreamed of ever writing a story like Mark Twain, he would have to find a balance between literacy and leisure. How was it possible to dream up the likes of Tom Sawyer and Huckleberry Finn without making it a point to regularly spend quality time with Mother Nature?

As our boy began warming up to her convincing, the teacher's mind became crowded with second thoughts. Was sending him outside really the right thing to do? If any of the big, bad wolves roaming the playground happened to be in a predatory mood that day, there was a good chance they might huff, puff, and blow our boy's newfound and precarious sense of self-esteem down, sending him back to square one or worse. Acutely aware that such an outcome would unravel all the progress she had made integrating the boy with his peers, she became hyper-protective and decided to present the boy with an alternate option to remain indoors and help her around the classroom. He would surely take her up on such an offer, and she would have peace of mind knowing he was safe. Yes, that was what she would do.

But before she could get the words out, one of the other boys from the reading club called down the hallway to our boy, inviting him to join the others outside. A shy, mild-mannered lad who had been bullied himself on occasion due to his plump physique, he implored our boy to mount his proverbial horse and hurry it up a little. Although it was most unusual for this particular boy, known more as a Beta, to exhibit such outgoing behaviour, his voluntary invitation to play filled the hearts of the teacher and our boy with tremendous joy.

In the teacher's case, this was irrefutable evidence that the strategy being employed to make life at school better for our outcast boy was working, billowing her soul's sails with a gust of intrinsic fulfillment, her most cherished means of compensation. Even though the chubby boy was far from being the most popular member of the exclusive reading club, the other students did respect his genius. He was a top academic performer and precocious orator from a highly respected family. And one friend for our boy was far better than zero. It was progress. It was a start.

Looking up at the teacher with bright-eyed wonder, as if silently asking to be pinched so he could prove to himself without a shadow of a doubt that he wasn't dreaming, our boy stood frozen, shocked that, not unlike the smog that had been lifted outside, the dark cloud that had shadowed him all his life was finally dissipating. He had made a friend. It didn't matter who it was. It felt incredible.

Seeing that she had to snap our boy out of his state of shock, the teacher, playing the role of a genie granting a wish, crossed her arms, smiled, and blessed his acceptance of the stout lad's invitation with a subtle tilt of her head. Upon receiving her signal, our boy came to his senses and sped for the doors leading to the playground at breakneck speed, while his new and first friend waved him forth, holding open the doors and beckoning him with great enthusiasm.

As our boy emerged into the schoolyard, the warmth and brightness of the sun enveloped him with life-giving energy. Closing his eyes for a moment as he ran, he felt as though he were being conveyed through the air by the soft breeze. Reopening his eyes, he spotted a large group of his most popular classmates, many of whom had never spoken a kind word to or about him, clustered together some distance away. Hooting and hollering, they cheered his approach and urged him to make haste, barely able to contain themselves. Not since running into his mother's arms had our boy been more eager to close a distance.

It is not an uncommon phenomenon to recall life's best moments as having gone by in fast-forward and life's worst moments as having gone by in slow motion, prompting us to rue the passage of time as unfair in both extremes. This is because, while things are happening in real time, the experience of life's highs and lows decreases or increases our awareness of the passage of time in accordance with the degree to which we enjoy or loathe that which we are experiencing. It is this very phenomenon that causes people to remember their wedding as having sped by in the blink of an eye. Conversely, it is this very phenomenon that causes people to remember time standing still after a devastating and unexpected break-up. In the first case, recollections take the form of a blur. In the latter, each painful detail, each torturous second, leaves an indelible imprint on our memory.

As our jubilant boy drew nearer to the beckoning group of children, he began to intuit something sinister in the expressions on their faces. There was a twinkle in their eyes that betrayed a menacing intent lying in wait behind their friendly façades, like a pack of wolves disguised as sheep, luring its prey until the moment was ripe to pounce. The process of coming to this realization brought time, as experienced through our boy's sensibilities, to a crawl. The entire scene slowed down and became distorted in his mind, the same way sound stretches out and deepens when a thumb presses down on a vinyl record. Beginning to understand that he had been deceived and was rushing headlong toward a trap, a sensation of numbness shot through both legs, causing him to trip and tumble onto an arid patch of ground, sending a plume of dust into the air around him. He had fallen head over heels in the worst possible manner, at the worst imaginable time.

Face-down and prone, our boy looked up and, through a cloud of red dust, saw the group of children walking toward him, cackling and egging one another on as they strode. Craning his neck, the boy looked behind himself in hopes of spotting a teacher on yard duty that might intervene to his rescue. All he could see, however, was the chubby kid who had shepherded him outside in the first place, frozen to the spot with a look of horror on his face, as if he knew not what he had done but was beginning to understand the part he had played in what was about to unfold. It's not unusual for victims of bullying to become patsies.

As he lay helplessly in the dirt, our boy found himself ensnared by his assailants. The mob encircled him, forming a Stonehenge of terror. Submissive and frightened, our boy recognized all the other kids from the book club among the glowering faces staring down at him. He couldn't hold back his tears any longer, shedding them in large droplets, each plowing a wet streak through the dust that had collected on his quavering cheeks.

After having worked themselves up into a crazed frenzy, the raving cluster of children reached a fever pitch of disdain for the pathetic, sniveling sack cowering in the fetal position at their feet. The pupils in their fiery eyes dilated, indicating an unchained madness brewing from within. Teeth gnashed and nostrils flared. Gang mentality caused otherwise innocent children to mutate into grotesque and diabolical creatures thirsting to feed mercilessly off the vulnerability of their victim. Hideousness incarnate.

Now sobbing uncontrollably, our frightened and vulnerable boy urinated himself for all his tormenters to see (and smell). An evolutionary last gasp effort to fend off predators by repelling them, all wetting his pants did for our boy was exhaust what little restraint the mob had remaining. With the maniacal look of someone who has lost all concept of consequences, one of the bigger, more braggadocious boys (the type starving for the approval of a punitive father) picked up a rock from the ground and raised it above his head. After letting out a tribal cry, he hurled the rock full force into the side of our helpless boy's rib cage. The first stone had been cast.

Stunned into momentary silence and stillness, the others glanced around at one another as though at a crossroads. Would they acknowledge that things had gone too far and back down, or would they pour fuel over the fire they saw burning in one another's eyes?

Before the voice of reason, always hesitant to speak up in a crowd setting, had the chance to intervene, a second boy (spoiled rotten by his family and ever eager to play follower to whoever he felt carried the most playground clout at any given point in time) hurled a second rock at our ailing boy, who was by then clutching his side and gasping in pain. Barely missing the boy's head, what the second stone did was unleash malevolence in the hearts of the other children. As if an invisible demonic force was jumping from child to child, a third boy launched a rock, followed by a fourth and a fifth. With no stone in hand, one of the girls stepped forth to spit on our now writhing boy, prompting a second girl to one-up her by kicking him squarely in the face. Blood streamed from his delicate nostrils.

And thus unfolded a chain reaction that escalated into a gang beating, the likes of which would have been unimaginable in an affluent, exclusive gated community until it occurred. As so often becomes the case in life, something "can never happen" until it does. None are immune.

Aside from the grunts and shrieks that our poor boy let out each time a running shoe forced the air from his lungs, he remained silent throughout the entire ordeal. Rather than begging for mercy or crying out for help, our boy instead retreated into his own mind, distracting himself from the agony being inflicted upon him by repeating an age-old lesson that his mother had instilled in him at a very young age: *sticks and stones may break my bones, but names will never hurt me*. In truth, it all hurt, but the thought of his mother soothed him as he drifted in and out of consciousness, his eyes rolling back in his head.

Teetering on the brink between his conscious mind and the subconscious universe, our boy could hear what sounded like a muffled and muddled voice crying out hysterically somewhere in the distance. At the same time, the cacophonous voices of his attackers dissolved and grew distant. A part of his mind vaguely signaled that the worst of the ambush was over. The tension that seizes every muscle when the body is under siege was released, leaving him a placid bag of bones.

Wincing as much from the brightness of the blue sky as from the physical agony that shot through his being, our ailing boy thought he could hear his mother calling out to him. Her soft and angelic voice echoed as if spoken in a vast and empty auditorium. It grew louder, closer. She reassured him that she was there now. Everything would be fine. She would protect him.

Our boy's surroundings then fell silent and faded to black. Freed from the confines of his body, he could still somehow see, but differently than with his eyes. His mother, translucent and shimmering, hovered an indistinct distance away. He wanted to stay in that happy and safe place with Mommy forever, never to return to his miserable earthly existence. The more this will expressed itself, the bigger and brighter a light of the most brilliant, indescribable colours expanded at the centre of the infinite void, representing the opening of a horizon from which there is no turning back.

Grazing the light's surface, our boy, for a brief moment, felt the entire wisdom of the universe and beyond course through him like a bolt of lightning. Before he had the opportunity to go any further, his mother intervened, prohibiting his passage. She explained that although his temporal existence was characterized by hardship, he was needed. His was a higher calling. He had to trust her and go back. She vowed to watch over him until it was time for them to be reunited forever.

Our boy's mother then fell silent and her image faded. Noise from the playground returned to the fore, as if the volume of life was being turned back on. The intense brightness of the sky pierced through our boy's eyelids. The dull aches and acute stings of each welt and wound returned with full fury, causing him to squirm in the dirt as if he wore a flaming straitjacket from which he could not escape. He could still hear a voice by his side, but it was no longer that of his mother. It was someone different. As his senses returned, he recognized it as the voice of his favourite teacher. She placed her hands gently on his shoulders.

With tremulously spoken words, she did her best to reassure him that he was safe and that help was on the way. Her hands trembled as she wiped away blood that constricted his breathing. Between attempts to soothe our boy with words, she called out to an unspecified source asking for an update. She implored our boy to stay right there with her, as if there were somewhere else he might go.

At long last, the blare of sirens could be heard approaching. Encouraged by the knowledge that help was close at hand, the teacher repeated reassuring phrases to our boy. Everything was going to be okay. They would be reading *The Prince and the Pauper* again in no time.

As she spoke, our boy, using all the might he could muster, opened his eyes a crack to stare the teacher directly in the face through his blurred vision. Recognizing that he was alert and trying to say something, the teacher paused, put her ear to the boy's mouth, and listened intently. Struggling mightily to speak, our boy uttered in no uncertain terms that he hated her and wished her dead.

Distraught, the teacher promised to make things right, but it was too late. The damage was done. The burning rage that sullies the souls of those who are wicked among us had already set in. Our boy's eyes, mirroring the change that had taken place in his heart, were already turning black.

III

In the years following the playground incident, our now teenage boy experienced even the sunniest days as overcast and bleak. His entire world had taken on a downcast aspect and dreary hue. Finding refuge in the shadows, he cloaked himself from what he came to view as the vain and superficial society around him. By day, he carried out an inconspicuous routine. Come nightfall, he became a regular Raskolnikov, brooding silently in the darkness, the scornful voice in his head railing louder and louder—and louder still—against his cruel and heartless species. He was a lone wolf, harbouring anger and resentment toward anyone and everyone for all the pain and suffering he had been forced to endure over the years. He was filled with a festering hatred that was ready to burst. Behind a façade of normalcy, great evil lay germinating in the form of vengefulness. The world would get what it had coming. He would teach human beings a lesson they would never forget.

A few years earlier, his foster parents had died within minutes of one another, as is so often the case when a couple bound by a lifetime of true love is finally separated by death in old age. As if Nature herself can't bear the sight of an elderly widow's or widower's fresh agony any longer, she quickly puts them out of their misery to ensure the couple's time apart is as brief as possible, and somewhere in an afterlife, they may resume where they left off. Coroners may make all the physiological determinations they wish to, but death that occurs mourning a lifelong soulmate is surely caused by a broken heart, not heart failure.

Had their adopted son been less closed off emotionally and opened himself up even a smidgen to their unconditional love for him, perhaps one or both could have stretched out a few more years of longevity. Instead, with nothing more to live for, they embraced the encroachment of death openly and as natural a process as birth.

Having had their heartfelt offers of emotional support spurned time and again, they left behind a form of support that even the most ascetic among us cannot fully eschew—money. A handsome trust fund had been set up in our boy's name that was not to be released until the angry and angst-ridden teenage boy reached the age of majority.

Our now adolescent boy was of two very conflicting minds concerning the passing of the elderly couple in whose custody and under whose guardianship he had been raised for all but the first few years of his life. On the one hand, they were not his parents. This was a biological fact he expressed on many an occasion through his defiant behaviour. Whether it was despondency, coldness in response to warmth and tenderness, or temperamental outbursts, his staunch resistance to their kindness produced an undeniable schism between him and his foster parents. Sickened by what he imagined to be their use of money to purchase his affection, he lived as meagrely as possible: he was not for sale—unless he really needed that cutting-edge computer or those high-end military boots. For the most part, however, our boy went to all lengths possible to establish and enforce strict boundaries between him and his caregivers. He made this abundantly clear every time he shut himself in his room for hours, even days, on end behind a padlocked door. It was all far more extreme than a typical adolescent struggle for greater privacy and independence. Toward the end, the most consistent and predictable time the three of them spent together was at the dining table, when exchanges of words were limited to practical considerations such as whether this condiment was desired or that serving would be enough. Any attempts to engage the boy in more in-depth or personal matters were either rebuffed with silence or curt reminders about what was and was not their business. The more pain his distance caused them, the better, for he was not their real son, and punishing them with a perennially cold shoulder was, he believed, the sole method at his disposal for making sure they never lost sight of that fact. In this regard, he didn't mourn the loss of his so-called parents. They were not that. Not even close. Nobody could replace his mother.

On the other hand, familiarity is a powerful thing. In the same way that victims of protracted abuse and captivity often display a counterintuitive attachment to their oppressors—a phenomenon that has come to be known as Stockholm syndrome—our boy, somewhere hiding beneath the calluses forming around his heart, wept for the loss of the only two real companions he had. Suppress it though he may, our boy experienced a profound and inescapable sense of loss when they died. And while it may not have fit the image of nihilistic antipathy he wished to convey, his grief refused to go away. Try as we may, we can never fully lie to ourselves. We can't shake the truth. There is no escaping emotion, only drowning it out or burying it. Somewhere trapped beneath an icy avalanche of indifference, the boy's muffled distress signals came through in faint murmurs of grief and sorrow.

The small fortune being held in trust for our boy stipulated the approval of any amount required to attend the private high school of his choice. With what felt like unlimited resources at his disposal, our boy chose the nearest private school he could find that would guarantee him his own, private dorm room. He would have to pay a little more, but it would be worth it. This afforded him the privacy and anonymity he required to incubate his *plan*.

Outwardly, every aspect of our boy's student persona was carefully constructed to create the appearance of normality. By blending in, he could effectively conceal the fact that he was plotting something sinister beneath the surface. His academic performance was a tad above average, not exceptional in any way. His spotless attendance record and orderly behaviour provided no grounds for the school's administration to take any special notice, let alone place him under a microscope. He was polite, handed in his assignments on time, asked and answered the odd question in class, and even volunteered to tutor students with special needs. He had a soft spot for them.

He was neither attractive enough to receive unwanted attention from girls nor disagreeable enough to elicit their ridicule. He spent his lunch hours poring over books, none of which were assigned reading. Never to be pushed around again, he spent not a small amount of time at the school gym. Barring the occasional coaxing to join the school sports teams, interactions between him and the other boys were limited to the odd nod of mutual recognition when crossing paths between classes. In the eyes of his high school peers, he was a harmless guy with a difficult past who wanted to be left alone, and there was no socially compelling reason not to respect that. He was different and an outsider, sure, but a target for disparagement he was not. In fact, he often wished to intervene in defense of other victims of bullying, but, reminding himself of the bigger picture, he would invariably decide that certain sacrifices would have to be made for the successful execution of his *plan*. He was focused on the war, not the battle. He had bigger fish to fry. So for now, he would simply blend in. When the time came, the world would have no choice but to take notice of him.

Upon returning to his private dorm room each day after school, our adolescent boy began his daily transformation. Peeling off his trendy clothing as if it were a skin not his own, he made haste to the shower, where he would exfoliate vigorously enough to draw blood. He did this to cleanse himself of the imagined scum that built up every time he was forced to keep up appearances in the pathetically shallow world beyond his dormitory walls. He was a sheep shearing its own coat. But the façade was both temporary and mandatory. It was all part of his *plan*, a plan he followed to the letter.

After purifying himself thusly, he would stand naked in front of the mirror, observing his body as it transmuted into the gnarled creature he convinced himself he had truly become. Twitching and distorting bit by bit, his facial features strained and contorted until he took on a glowering, menacing countenance. His posture shifted from that of a statuesque young man to a lurching invertebrate. His hands coiled up in a deranged, arthritic manner, resembling brittle autumn leaves curled on the ground. To one who believed in such things, this transfiguration could quite easily be mistaken for demonic possession. Part of his deranged behaviour was symptomatic of an overwhelming amount of unresolved inner trauma. The other part of it was a thespian performance he put on to encourage his own conviction.

After this ritual, he was ready to resume the painstaking, obsessive plotting that consumed his every waking moment outside of school. He would dress in all black and order delivery food to sustain himself while he wrote well into the early hours of the morning. He was drafting a full-length manuscript he referred to as his *Manifesto*. In a nondescript room furnished with little more than the necessities characteristic of a military barrack, he sat at the computer every night with no light to aid his vision save for the glow from the monitor, upon which his eyes remained fastidiously fixed until he couldn't hold them open any longer.

He wrote in painstaking detail about an evil blight blanketing the earth, a widespread scourge that left nothing but death and carnage in its wake. If left unchecked, this pestilence would soon wipe out most of the organic life on the planet, taking its own existence in the process, just like any other plague. He knew this because he belonged to the plague—he was a human being.

On the nature of man, our author was as unforgiving as he was relentless. Human beings were the inventors and sole practitioners of sin. To harry, rape, pillage, steal, deceive, murder, bully, and demean were shared tendencies buried deep within the marrow of their bones. Annihilation was their driving force. They were at the root of all the world's problems. People were by far the most destructive misfits to have ever evolved from the great primordial soup, yet they believed themselves to be God's proudest creation. Did God create man in His own image or vice versa?

Human were, as a rule, corrupt and villainous. When temptation presented itself in the form of a charming snake showcasing a sparkling apple in its coiled tail, these weakest of primates succumbed without batting an eye. If they could get away with breaking laws and abandoning their integrity, they would. Even if they couldn't, that mightn't be enough to stop them from trying. Not one among their entire species was unshakably bound to morality, no matter how saintly their act or sterling their reputation. This was the nature of Homo sapiens.

The same clergyman who assigned penitence to a man who confessed to stealing bread in order to feed his son regularly used the penitent man's son to feed his own sick sexual proclivities. The legislator who passed harsher penalties for tax evasion dipped her free hand in the public coffers while she scribed. The officer responsible for serving and protecting the public privately encased his mistress in cement. In each case, chained up and hissing in a cavernous dungeon, where the shadows of devils dance to flickering torches, the scaly, slimy *Id* slithered free from its shackles to fulfill a forbidden desire, only to return of its own accord and resume its feigned struggle in submissive captivity, as if it had been there all along. *Shh*. No one had to know.

The only species with a concept of evil was its most skilled practitioner. Which came first, chicken or egg? And like pointillism, individual sins made isolated marks that bore no pattern until the totality of those marks was zoomed out upon to reveal a self-portrait of man in all its diabolical horror. Man was a disgrace to the animal kingdom.

The global scientific community was and had for generations been in agreement that humans were the single greatest threat to life on earth, but not even the unanimous consensus of top experts at observing and explaining natural phenomena was sufficient cause for the collective acceptance, introspection, and action required to divert what was a runaway train on a collision course with mass extinction.

Evidence of the carnage being left in humanity's wake was not in short supply. The biosphere had been chronically ill for some time and was deteriorating rapidly. In addition to its high fever, it suffered from a laundry list of ailments as long as, if the pun can be excused, the Dead Sea Scrolls. Forests were being felled at the rate of a small country per year; oceans were fast becoming acidic and inhospitable; delicate ecosystems and habitats were being contaminated in higher and higher concentrations. On and on it went, and all of it as if turning a blind eye negated consequence.

The earth's immune system was no different than those of the many species whose lives it supported. In addition to a rapidly rising fever, she heaved, quaked, and sweated with increasing intensity in desperate bids to rid herself of a pathogen whose skill at proliferation and consumption was unmatched in all of nature. Wildfires and other natural disasters raged with increasing frequency and force. These were all symptoms of a grave systemic malady. The mother of all life was suffering from late-stage metastatic cancer.

But to reach that point had been a slow and painful decline, taking place over many generations. Consequently, billions upon billions of humans had lived and been buried in the ground they helped taint before the truly apocalyptic effects of their devastating aggregate impact became known. They were great inventors, but neglected and let languish their gift of foresight. Tomorrow wasn't their concern; it wasn't their problem. They would be dead long before the conditions required to sustain organic life finally collapsed.

So who was culpable? None, it seemed. It was only a matter of time until the camel's back broke and some unfortunate and helpless future generation inherited a barren wasteland beset by widespread famine, plague, and conflict.

Rather than join forces in a collective attempt to reverse or at least curtail the momentum they had built toward their own untimely fate, humans of this colour or that belief or that sociocultural affiliation seethed with hatred and railed with anger against one another simply because they were "different." Paradoxically, they despised each other for the one thing they all had in common—variation. *Those who aren't like me are the enemy* was their intolerant credo. The greater the difference, the greater the cause for discrimination, disparagement, and, in many cases, persecution. On a small scale, it was the orphan being bullied in the schoolyard. On a large scale, it was the Holocaust. *If you don't look like, think like, or act like me, chances are we have a problem.*

And so, in a world in which bridges were so desperately needed to address an impending calamity, petty and small-minded Homo sapiens the world over carried on in the same old manner: building walls and carving out borders to create and maintain rigid divisions between themselves, effectively fragmenting the whole of the human race into an enormous and scattered jigsaw puzzle that was far too daunting to attempt piecing together. Where would one even begin?

As crises of their own making worsened and the threat of annihilation loomed on the fast approaching horizon, humanity numbed itself with a wider and wider selection of distracting technological toys and pleasurable pursuits to insulate itself from and drown out the deafening and agonizing cries of the writhing and withering planet around them. Entertaining themselves to death, indeed.

Etc. Etc. Etc. Our boy wrote page after page of scathing indictments, tearing his own species to shreds.

Feeling irredeemably victimized in his own life, our despondent and vindictive teenager clung to existential threats such as the worsening environmental crisis as proof positive that the very species that had ruined his life was also leaving all life in ruins. He saw himself as an exception, as much a victim of human beings as was the planet. He felt this to be a sound justification to lash out and make a statement of grand proportions. It would be his dire warning to the world. It would also force the world to acknowledge how truly powerful the once forgotten and discarded little boy had become.

It was in this warped state of mind that our disturbed boy came to believe that he himself had been handpicked to serve a greater purpose. He had been chosen to speak up on behalf of those victims who didn't yet have a voice with which to defend themselves. He thought of himself as the present-day guerrilla leader of future generations. Those who, as yet unborn, were unable to prevent the wretched conditions they would inherit from their predecessors.

As self-appointed spokesperson, our boy was convinced beyond the point of dissuasion that his life's primary objective was to indict, convict, and punish human beings for committing *crimes against posterity*, a phrase he had coined one night as he lay awake brooding in bed.

No matter how preposterous and far-fetched a delusion of grandeur this all was, our boy believed it to be real. And, as is made evident from the countless examples that surround us on a daily basis, humans are woefully inept at distinguishing their beliefs from reality.

Seeing it as his destiny to trigger the dawn of a great popular uprising, our twisted boy would see his *plan* through, come hell or high water. In fact, he welcomed the former in order to prevent the latter. He wanted to die. He needed to. It was integral to his *plan*. Only through death could he be assured that his name, ideas, and broader vision would be widely circulated and taken up by the masses. He would be a martyr. Vilified at first, but later revered and canonized for his sacrifice and courage.

Ensuring his *Manifesto* was broadcast widely would be a cinch. Every little detail about his life would be reported on to the point of exhaustion by an impulsive, desperate, instantaneous, and impossible-to-regulate Press. They couldn't help themselves. The kind of news our boy would make was just the sort the news media craved. He would make a name for himself, and it would be the last thing he did. The only thing being remembered and worshipped would cost him was his life.

The *Manifesto* was how our boy planned on recruiting his army. It would awaken millions of would-be militia men and women who, thirsting for an excuse to unite and rise up for the cause, would be first to the front lines the moment his dog whistle sounded. Guided by the militant directions he was to leave behind, his followers, loyal and brave, would solemnly dedicate the remainder of their lives to protecting the future of the planet in his hallowed name. His words would be recited as gospel, as timeless scripture that would inspire the emergence of a new and better era.

In our boy's warped, misanthropic mind, his death would secure his immortality and set the tone for a legacy that would represent a turning point in humanity's slow procession toward its own funeral. The hypnotized mainstream might detest him in the short term, but when the revolution eventually took hold, he'd be admired and revered for all time as not only the savior of the future of his species, but the future of life itself. Our boy fantasized that like Galileo before him, his name would go from reviled to universally celebrated once the new paradigm he set in motion forced humans to accept that they weren't situated at the centre of the solar system after all.

Each night as he typed away furiously, his eyes set ablaze and grew wild with the fiery passion that fueled his disturbing and maniacal pursuit. As his thoughts accelerated, the rambling words and mostly incoherent phrases seemed to write themselves, as if he'd become possessed. At the keyboard, he considered himself a maestro in the vein of a Mozart or Beethoven, playing to an imagined auditorium where the rows stretched on infinitely, as far as the mind's eye could see. His genius would not go unnoticed. His purpose would not go unfulfilled.

The more his vision took shape, the more certain he became in the perverted belief that his wicked impulses were actually prophetic signals ordaining him to carry out a divine act, as if he himself, of the billions of humans who had been granted the mysterious and miraculous occasion to breathe air in this life, were truly Heaven's preferred messenger. Madness had taken over.

One night, after months and hundreds of thousands of assiduously crafted words, he put the final touches on his radical *Manifesto* and stored a copy of it on his computer where it could easily be found by the authorities. Every measure had to be taken to guarantee the plan was carried out to the letter. Tomorrow marked the long anticipated big day. All of his hard work would finally bear fruit. Death's long, icy fingers hovered above his tense shoulders.

Wrapping up earlier than he had grown accustomed to during his long run of sleepless nights, our misguided insomniac became filled with a distorted sense of accomplishment and pride. The anticipation was almost too much to bear. Left with nothing more to do but wait for time to pass, he tucked himself into bed in a hopeless attempt to catch a few hours' sleep. Far from feeling as though he needed rest (considering the eternal horizon of slumber that awaited him), he was simply feeling impatient and wanted to make the night pass more quickly. Unable to keep his eyes closed let alone sink into the abstract abyss of his subconscious mind, the boy's night vision adapted to the room's darkness to the extent that he could make out its shapes and shadows.

As he lay motionless, his mind wandered freely. After some moments, his thoughts transported him to a previous occasion during which his excitement regarding the following day's events had kept him from falling asleep. It was during elementary school, when he found out he had been selected by his favourite teacher to take part in her exclusive reading club. He stood at the foot of the bed in his room at his foster parents' house, watching his younger self toss and turn restlessly from one side of the pillow to the other in eager anticipation. He reached out toward the bed to reassure himself it wasn't real.

The moment his hand was about to make contact with the sleepless child's bare foot, he was suddenly and violently whisked away and thrown tumbling across a cold and damp classroom where his younger self sat cross-legged among a group of motionless children with pale, featureless faces. The now maligned schoolteacher sat atop a stone throne towering hundreds of feet above them, her words garbled and unintelligible.

In unison, the ghostly children rose slowly to their feet and surrounded our boy's younger self. The teacher cackled wildly from her lofty perch. Our boy screamed at them to stop. It was at this point that one of the demonic little imps noticed our boy's older self and turned a blank face in his direction. The other goblin children followed suit, turning their heads one by one until they were all directing their empty gazes his way. Our boy's younger self buried his face in his lap and covered his ears. The number of demon children began to multiply. There were dozens, hundreds, thousands of them, rising to their feet and converging on him. Frozen and no longer able to produce sound, he closed his eyes and braced for the worst.

With a visceral and spastic jerk, our teenage boy found himself sitting up in bed with his covers bunched up over his legs, sweating and gasping for breath. It had all been a dream.

Collecting his thoughts while his heart rate returned to normal, he glanced at his watch, only to realize to his furious chagrin that he had overslept. He was late. He rolled out of bed and hastily went through his exhaustive preparatory checklist. That poor excuse for a teacher had already ruined his life. He'd be damned if she got in the way of his destiny, too.

Under the gun, as it were, he skipped showering and wore what he had slept in, reasoning that a day's build-up of dirt and bacteria was just a head start on the long process of biological decay and decomposition that awaited him in no more than a few hours' time.

A fan of his own dark sense of humour until the last, he snickered sardonically while assembling the instrument required to carry out the next part of his *plan*. Once the guitar case into which it had been packed was fastened, he lifted the case to test that it was secure and realized it was much heavier than he expected. He laced up his leather boots, buttoned up his long winter coat, and left his dorm for the last time, looking like a young musical talent setting out to make a name for himself.

Off he went, trudging through the snow-blanketed park that acted as a shortcut between his dorm and his final destination. He couldn't help but observe how clean and pure nature was anywhere humans hadn't yet had the chance to contaminate it. Aside from a few footprints left by rodents traveling between trees, it was a pristine, angelic white.

The snow that had the misfortune of landing on the adjacent major avenue, on the other hand, was a black and tarry toxic slush. Having soaked up emissions and pollutants to the point of saturation, the snow on the road had become a cancerous lung, repulsive to the eye, but not enough to deter the behaviour that caused it. When spring arrived, this poisonous runoff would melt, draining into sewers and leaching into neighbouring habitats for all to enjoy.

If a shred of uncertainty remained somewhere in our boy's mind concerning what he was about to do, this well-timed snapshot of humans' shameful disregard for the natural world extinguished it for good. They had to be stopped. His destiny must be fulfilled.

As his train of thought raced along thusly, something most unexpected occurred that challenged our boy's resolve. From somewhere nearby in the park came the muffled sobs of a young woman. He managed to ignore the sound at first, but it eventually permeated his impenetrable exterior, striking a tender chord he had worked so hard to keep buried away. The sensation produced by this unexpected emotional breach quite literally stopped him in his tracks. He commanded himself to ignore it, but something inside him remained defiant. What harm was a thirty-second detour?

After a few moments of mental tug-of-war, our boy sighed, muttered about how foolish he was being, and walked over to quickly inspect the matter before resuming his fateful mission.

Rounding a hedgerow, he found a distraught damsel sitting alone on a bench at the base of an ancient tree. The moment he laid eyes on her, a rush of excitement ran through him. His skin tingled and its little hairs stood on end. It was as if the branches swaying in the breeze overhead were a cluster of magic wands casting a spell on him. Whatever was happening, it was powerful enough to temporarily disable years of pent up rage. He was mesmerized. In the blink of an eye, he had completely forgotten himself. As if hypnotized, our boy stared at the striking woman weeping before him.

He decided he would ask if she was okay. That was all. Nothing more. Then he would be on his way.

As he made his approach, doing his best not to startle her, one of his steps snapped a twig that lay hidden beneath the snow's surface. The young woman quickly drew her hands away from her swollen eyes to see what had caused the sound. Realizing a young man had been watching her cry when she thought she had been alone, she let out a gasp. In response, he stood motionless with one leg raised in the air like a deer that has been spotted and is unsure how to proceed.

Speaking with such anxious rapidity that he stumbled over his words, our boy frantically explained that he meant no harm, was sorry to have frightened her, and only wanted to make sure everything was okay, and that he would leave now, and was terribly sorry, and just wanted to make sure she was okay and all. After this went on for what felt like an eternity, he trailed off inaudibly to his own obvious embarrassment. *Idiot*, he thought.

Mortified at the situation he had got himself into, our boy's inner voice castigated him for being so weak. The culmination of his life's work awaited him literally around the corner. It was the holiday season. The festive market was a block away and in full swing. It would be packed with people and all manner of goods, including sitting ducks and fish in barrels. This was no time for stage fright. He didn't need any eleventh-hour distractions to jeopardize his magnum opus. His unsuspecting audience awaited his overture.

While our boy was thusly consumed, the young woman was collecting her own thoughts. There was something about the awkward young man who appeared out of nowhere when she was at her most vulnerable that set her stricken heart aflutter. That he had noble intentions and was checking to make sure she was okay was as clear as the day, but equally evident was his bashfulness. If ever they were to move beyond the uneasy impasse at which they found themselves, she would have to take control of the situation. Nodding at the guitar case by his side as she wiped away tears with her woolen mittens, she asked him if he played. She was half hoping he would answer yes, not through words, but by serenading her with a song to raise her spirits.

Unsure how or if to respond, our boy, utterly conflicted at this point, looked at her in confusion. Just as he was about to lie and say that it was a guitar he was returning to a friend, his pride ordered him to cut the nonsense along with his losses and get back to the execution of his *plan*. That was an order.

Without so much as a word in response to the young woman's question, our boy picked up the guitar case, performed an about-face, and walked away as quickly as possible without breaking into a run. He stumbled and fell knee first into the snow not a few times as he made his awkwardly hurried retreat, as if trying to escape himself as much as the situation.

Just when he thought the coast was clear and his *plan* was back on track, he heard the young woman calling out to him. Looking over his shoulder, what he saw stopped him mid-stride: refusing to allow their encounter to conclude as a meaningless crossing of paths in a chaotic world, she was hailing and running after him.

Once she caught up with him, she stopped and spoke with the crackled and congested voice of one who had been shedding tears for hours on end. She wondered if he might, maybe, you know, want to grab a bite to eat with her some time, or something. Perhaps even later that day if he was free and up to it.

Furious with the relentlessness of this unexpected and unwelcome threat to his *plan*, our boy's inner voice scolded him for so much as considering the invitation. He was to stay his course, and that was final. He had worked too hard to throw it all away at the eleventh hour. And for what, a girl? Had he forgotten how cruel the world had been to him? She would hurt him, too. Just like everyone else. Had he forgotten his messianic purpose to deliver his own species from—and cure it of—itself? *Sally forth, revolutionary soldier! Let not the trivialities of superficial daily living stand between you and history. The bigger picture depends on you and you alone. The future of life itself lies in your... in your hands.*

He hesitated.

IV

Infatuation is a mighty intoxicant whose only possible antidote, Time, cannot guarantee it will effectively counteract it. Its dizzying spell has the power to entrance the strongest amongst us. Playing matchmaker while blindfolded and armed with arrow and bow, it aimlessly strikes its unsuspecting victims in the same way children sightlessly attempt to pin tails on donkeys. Neither all the reason nor all the logic in all the land can talk sense into those who have been placed under its spell. Infatuation renders us incorrigible. Only a phantom hypnotist deriving sick satisfaction from playing puppet master with our emotions has the power to awaken us from our stupefied trance once he, with a snap of his fingers, decides it's time. If and when he does, and only then, can the clouds of infatuation clear and our true feelings take root and be fully understood. In most cases, the result of post-infatuation clarity is heartache, regret, disaster, or a combination thereof.

But every so often, infatuation can set the stage for a love as true as the timeless romanticism of fairy tales. Happily-ever-after may be rare, but it is real. It is possible. Until the ends have justified the means, however, all is naught in matters of the heart. It is but a game of chance, a roll of the dice, or spin of the wheel—a love lottery for which we can only cross our fingers and hope.

That fateful snowy day, as our boy traversed the park with the intention of taking numerous lives he had never met, Oberon, king of the fairies, had different plans. When our boy least expected it and without notice, the mischievous elven monarch sprang out from behind the bushes and sprinkled infatuation-inducing dust onto his eyelids, guaranteeing he would fall headlong for the next person who crossed his path. How else, he marveled to himself, could he account for the absorbing immediacy of the attraction he felt toward an unknown young woman crying to herself on a park bench? From one moment to the next, he went from seeing red to viewing the world through rose-coloured lenses, a sea change that would forever alter the course of how he would see change. All it took was for another sad and solitary individual to defrost his heart. In an instant, he shed his deep-seated anger and resentment. His chronic emotional pain and scarring lifted as if a crippling rheumatism had, at once and of a sudden, gone into remission. His fixation with death was supplanted by a will to live; an involuntary smile took the place of a longstanding scowl. He was smitten.

Whether it had been predestined or was simply a coincidental stroke of dumb luck, the feeling was mutual. Each experienced that pull of irresistible magnetism that even the most chaste amongst us inevitably succumb to. Neither had any choice but to explore their feelings further. Whether it would lead to true love or heartache and disappointment remained to be seen.

One of the first things our young man learned about this intriguing young woman was the source of her profound distress. Sitting across from her later that same evening at a run-of-the-mill deli during what was, even if unofficially, his first-ever date, he listened intently and fidgeted restlessly while she described a most devastating recent personal tragedy. Her twin sister and best friend, the person with whom she shared her entire genome and innermost secrets, not to mention her desires and ambitions, died after an incurably aggressive cancer had agonizingly colonized enough of her body's healthy tissue to suffocate the last vestiges of her life. She couldn't believe she was sharing this with him right off the bat, but she hadn't really had many friends outside of her sister, and she had to talk to someone. She knew it wasn't healthy to just bottle everything up, and something about him made her feel comfortable, as if she'd known him in a previous life. She was sorry if it was too much information. But she wasn't sorry. She just didn't want to scare him away, was all. This, he silently echoed.

As she became more comfortable and confident in the situation, she began speaking with an eloquence and command that only served to further elevate her status in our boy's esteem. She was effortless in her impressiveness. As she spoke, he couldn't help but compare the way he felt in that moment with the way he had felt mere hours earlier. While it is not unusual for an individual to look back on an erstwhile period in his life and find it difficult to reconcile that version of himself with the present one, our boy had difficulty recognizing who he had been earlier that same day. "See how elastic our stiff prejudices grow when once love comes to bend them," Herman Melville whispered silently in our young man's literary remembrance.

The more our young man learned about and from the young woman sitting across the table from him, the more he understood her in a way that helped him better understand himself. He was not alone in the world after all. He was not the sole victim of profound sadness. Contrary to what he had so stubbornly held to be true, he was not unique in his misery. Everybody carried baggage. Just like him, she had experienced pain, loss, sorrow, alienation, and all their residual and relentless suffering. Just like him, she was highly intelligent and concerned with the many threats facing the planet. But there was an optimism about her that shone light where he had previously only ever known shadows and darkness.

In her bright, bloodshot eyes, what he saw staring back at him was hope. Hope for him. Hope for love. Hope for tomorrow. This was more than an endorphin-induced temporary sabbatical from an otherwise evil predisposition. It was more than the foolhearted excitement of a young man experiencing the thrills of romantic interest for the first time. There was some of that, to be sure, but this was something different, something more. He felt it. He believed it. This was a revelation that things could be better, that life could take on an entirely different direction. New, exciting scenarios for the future began to dance across in his imagination. He was no longer shut off from the prospect of happiness, and it felt sublime.

It didn't hurt that he also found her irresistibly attractive; more than the needle of his moral compass had shifted. Whereas popular views at the time concerning what made women eye-catching might have differed, the eyes of this beholder beheld beauty incarnate. She was an angel who, for reasons he failed to understand, had condescended to the realm of mortals, and even more perplexingly, had taken a shining to him, of all people. He was captivated. He pinched his thigh at intervals to remind himself he wasn't dreaming.

As he splashed about distractedly in the pool of his ponderings, it dawned on our young man that he had better return his undivided attention to the present, lest his, dare we say it—date!—catch him not listening, take offence, and storm out, never to look back. As is the case in the earliest stages of any budding romance, the fear that one wrong move will cause it all to unravel was ever-present. He worried that she was too good for him and it was only a matter of time until she realized it and abandoned him, reopening the very wounds she was in the process of helping to heal. Even the fleeting thought of her rejection caused him to shudder. She could make him or break him.

It was at this moment that our young man felt something bumping into his boots beneath the table. Thinking it might be a rodent, he recoiled his leg and bent over to investigate. What he discovered was a broom wielded by a minimum-wage-earning pubescent clerk who was passive-aggressively hinting that it was time to leave.

Already a half-step ahead in taking the hint, the young lady began reaching for her wallet. Unwilling to allow the opportunity for such an easy show of chivalry pass him by, our young Casanova insisted on paying. When she feigned a protest, he stood his ground, and she gave in. With blushing cheeks betraying gratitude for what, to her, was an overwhelming act of kindness and generosity, she thanked him effusively. She lowered her voice and let him know how much it meant to her. He bashfully replied that it was nothing. They then went silent, broke their protracted eye contact, and exhaled deep, simultaneous sighs.

With both the tab and their nerves settled, they made their way to the door, each silently fretting over how things might be left and whether the other was equal in their hope to schedule a second rendezvous. How unbridgeable is the gulf between two minds!

Although he had long questioned the wisdom in the unspoken Ladies First rule, wondering if perhaps it were nothing more than a cleverly designed way to secure a free and socially acceptable peek at a woman's behind, our young man, conscientiously doing his best to prevent any missteps, rushed to the door and held it open that she may pass through into the frosty night air without having to unnecessarily exert an ounce of upper body strength or expose her delicate hands to the germ-laden door handle. As the young woman accepted this most courtly gesture, she accidentally stepped on our young man's toes, lost her balance, and began falling through the doorway.

Quick to react from a combination of his proximity and hyper-attentiveness in the moment, our young man grabbed hold of the tumbling damsel's jacket in time to break her fall. After holding her in suspended animation for a moment while they both processed what had just taken place, he pulled her back to her feet and they burst into laughter at the narrowly averted catastrophe.

As they stood mere inches apart in the open doorway, the mood changed. The pair fell silent and serious. Their surroundings disappeared as they became lost in one another's eyes for a fraction of time that, to them, spanned multiple infinities. With pounding hearts, an irresistible gravitational pull drew them nearer and nearer by degrees until they, as if rehearsed over the course of tens of thousands of years of human evolution, shut their eyes at the same time and began to close the gap separating their mouths.

The instant before their lips met, the sound of a most unwelcome voice wedged itself between them. As if part of his job description were to spoil the experience of patrons, it was the clerk, this time barking at them to take it outside and close the door behind them. Didn't they know it was the dead of winter and they were letting in the cold?

Losing their nerve after being mere millimeters from officially sealing their shared affection, the would-be lovers stiffened up and fidgeted about clumsily before exiting, lady first. As the door was closing behind him, our now frustrated and embarrassed young man left the clerk an additional tip in the form of a trailing middle finger.

Their self-protective guards back up, the pair stood at arm's length beneath a streetlamp, exchanging pleasantries while their minds filled like adjacent sinks with uncertainties and doubts. Feeling defeated and unable to take the lead, our deflated young man, visibly shrinking in stature, extended his arm outward for history's most cringeworthy handshake.

Wrongly interpreting it as a cue that her feelings were unreciprocated, the humiliated young lady accepted his hand in hers, thanked him for the meal and the conversation, and walked away in the manner of a soldier who has been disgracefully discharged from service. As she went her separate way, she chastised herself for revealing so much to a stranger who likely spent the entire date wondering when it would be over but was too polite to say anything.

As her outline shrank in the distance, so, too, did our young man's hopes. It was his latest reminder that his sole purpose in life was to be on the receiving end of misery. Rejection followed him everywhere he went; sorrow was his only loyal companion. It was further evidence that he had always been and would forever be an outsider looking in. Only this time, the reminder of his inescapably pathetic lot in life failed to reignite his anger and resentment toward the world around him. This time, he felt numb. Nothing mattered. He resolved to end it all that night. Quietly. Privately. All he wanted was to die.

Paces away from an alleyway into which he would once again withdraw from society, our young man heard rapidly approaching footsteps. Someone was coming for him. Glancing over his shoulder to assess the situation, he clenched his fists in anticipation of a would-be attacker he would be more than happy to thrash to a pulp. Whoever this mysterious assailant was, they had chosen the wrong guy at the wrong time in the wrong place. Our young man was in such a state of despair that not even the most hardened or desperate criminal could possibly have had less to lose than he.

Ready for anything, he stood his ground as the silhouette bearing down on him emerged into the streetlight to reveal its identity. To his welcome astonishment, it was no delinquent stirring up mischief. Quite the opposite. It was the young woman he'd been certain had walked out of his life forever. He relaxed his fists.

Determined to prevent the only brush with love she'd ever had from slipping away, she had returned of her own accord. Opportunity had knocked, and she was prepared to do everything in her power to answer its call.

It was at that moment that our boy got his first taste of her indomitable will.

She flung herself upon him, wrapping her arms around his neck and straddling his torso with her legs. Crying and laughing, she clung to him for dear life, muffling his attempts to communicate that he couldn't breathe. Indeed, she had taken his breath away in all senses of the phrase. Still barnacled to his body, she drew back her face in order that they may behold one another in their shared state of elation. Seeing tears in her eyes, our young man involuntarily shed his own, much in the same way a yawn leaps invisibly from one person to the next. Their mutual joy would not—could not—be contained.

Knowing full well they couldn't remain in that pose forever, our young man, his arms and back beginning to tire, started to tell her as much. Before he could finish his sentence, she shed whatever inhibitions remained and disabled his ability to speak any further by pressing her moistened lips onto his, triggering a storybook kiss that, if viewed from the top floor of a nearby building, would have looked like a scene from a settled snow globe. Losing all sense of space and time in their rapture, the pair eventually teetered to and fro before collapsing upon the snow-covered walkway into a heap of hysterical amusement.

After disentangling themselves, the lovestruck duo got back to their feet and dusted the snow from their clothing. Filled with the confidence that comes with the knowledge of a requited sentiment, their mood shifted from playful to intense. Their expressions softened and their voices lowered. Their surroundings disappeared.

As they chatted under their breath, the young woman caught a sudden chill from the bitter wind, causing her to shiver. Our young man surrendered himself to the moment and drew her under his arm where she could nestle in the warmth of his broad embrace. Gazing into his eyes with a look of amazement, she reached up and squeezed his nose before breaking into an adorable giggle. Her hands felt their way around his face to make sure he was real and that it wasn't all just a dream.

She was wise enough to know that it was best to take things slowly. According to every relationship article she had ever read, it was she, the woman, who must determine the tempo. By delaying gratification and leaving him wanting more, she was investing in their long-term viability. She wasn't about to mess it up for a quick thrill. Be not greedy; make thine cup last.

It was with these very thoughts governing her mind that the young lady politely declined our young man's offer to walk her home safely. When he reacted disappointedly, she knew she had him. But she also knew it was cruel to toy with him. She quickly quelled his anxiety by explaining that she hadn't very far to go and that her route was both well-lighted and very public. She'd be fine. She did, however, insist that he contact her the following morning to let her know when their next date would be and what it would entail. The ball was in his court.

Without missing a beat, he obediently acquiesced by bowing and spreading out his arms in the manner of a servant complying with his master. O, Confidence, great giver of strength and instant injection of self-assuredness!

There would be a second date.

V

To state that our young man and the young woman who was now *his* young woman—and he *her* young man—to state that they had each met the other's match would be to make an understatement of astronomical proportions. On the purely physical front—and back—they could not possibly have been more made for one another. Their waltzing pheromones, acting as erotic messenger fairies, carried a steady stream of delight to their respective olfactory systems. Just being in each other's presence unleashed a deluge of stimulating endorphins that could give any street drug a run for its money. As if concocted by Aphrodite herself, these natural uppers set their skin abuzz from head to toe, rendering futile any attempts to resist the forces of nature.

Not that they even for a moment considered resisting. They indulged as frequently as time and physiology permitted—sometimes daily, sometimes hourly…and sometimes for our overexcited and no longer virginal young man, no time between was required at all. In their heightened state, they were whisked away to a faraway place where, well, the explicit details of what took place are best left to the imagination, but suffice it to say that our young lovers enjoyed themselves on not a few occasions.

From an emotional standpoint, they wove together equal parts darkness and light, fusing yin and yang in perfect balance. In the same way the folds of their flesh would become indistinguishable in their rapture, their life forces merged eternal, forging an indestructible spiritual bond. Their shared understanding of loneliness made it impossible to take each other's company for granted. On the rare occasions when they were forced to be apart, they remained connected through their unfaltering devotion, such was their inextricable entanglement as quantum particles in a boundless universe.

They always extended to one another their undivided attention, including during the deafening stillness of protracted silence. In due course, the layers of their sweetly mutual understanding made baklava seem superficial by comparison. Their emotional openness allowed them to explore everything from the sadness of a despairing past to the euphoria of a wondrous present and the promise of a future untold. From the slightest twitch of the brow to a barely traceable change in the inflection of speech, they understood one another through and through. They even developed their own, personal linguistic code—a cipher—that only they, of all the earth's inhabitants, could understand. They were the definition of simpatico. Inside and out, two had become one. They had found true love.

How, one might be inclined to ask, could this have been true? How could our young man's heart have shifted so suddenly, drastically, and diametrically from cold and hard to warm and tender?

Although a seeming contradiction of character for a young man who not long ago seethed with repugnance toward his own species, unbendingly hell-bent on leaving devastation and suffering in his wake, the two extremes of malevolent misanthrope and benevolent benefactor can, paradoxically, be reconciled. Similar to how Nietzsche's atheist hatched from the protective confines of a puritanical egg after having been left disappointed by unanswered questions of faith, our young man's limitless capacity to love and care for the world around him had been jaded by a cruel and uncompromising life that rewarded his inherent good nature with an unceasing onslaught of tragedy and trauma. In the former case, the source of disillusionment was a higher power that failed to live up to its billing; in the latter case, it was humanity. Left unchecked, disenchanted individuals such as these tumble and spiral further and further down the rabbit hole until, eventually, they reach the point of no return, disavowing that which they had held to an unrealistic standard, and mutating into Jabberwockies forever trapped on the other side of Alice's looking glass.

If, however, the right inspiration should come along to intervene and prevent lost souls such as these from floating irretrievably into cynical nothingness, as do the safety tethers of astronauts, the fading embers of their former selves can be rekindled into a renewed optimism and accompanying desire to yet again lead a righteous life. For our young man, *she* was that inspiration. Thanks to *her*, he had been born again.

It's not that his beliefs about his own species' inherent tendency toward self-annihilation had changed. Far from it. He simply no longer used those beliefs as a justification for exacting revenge on a world that had been so unfair to him. Now that he had been acquainted with happiness and its accompanying desire to live, there was no longer a score to settle. Now that he had found love, his all-consuming bitterness and anger were a thing of the past.

Because his past—long an inescapable torment—no longer felt as if it belonged to him, our young man fabricated an alternate story about his upbringing in which he had been orphaned from birth and had since led a relatively normal and happy life characterized by the strong filial bond he developed with his late foster parents. In weaving this tall tale, he both closed the door to a lifetime of painful memories and shielded himself from the embarrassment he associated with them. The mere thought of our young lady knowing the truth about his background caused him to shudder with embarrassment. He was born trash and had ungratefully shunned the benevolent souls that had taken him in and loved him without condition. Surely this knowledge would cause her to see him in a lesser light and risk forever tarnishing him in her eyes. And so he kept the truth under lock and key, vowing to never again let it glimpse the light of day. Everyone was entitled to one dark secret, right? What she didn't know couldn't hurt her. That part of him was dead and buried now. He would be transparent about all else. (Like with any lie, his conscience slowly and persistently gnawed away at him, a self-inflicted parasite that burrowed deeper into his mind each time he failed to observe the maxim that honesty is the best policy.)

She was all that mattered to our young man, and he wouldn't allow yesterday's scars to get in the way. If she so desired, he'd readily have buried his most sacred and closely held values and beliefs to appease her. For better or for worse, he was prepared to play chameleon to the climes of her whims. His fear of losing her reigned supreme. Had she suggested they go on a pollution spree, he'd not have resisted. He'd have unhesitatingly asked when and where to meet, and then experienced an immense amount of stress not about the fact that he was forsaking his own ideals, but over what to wear and say.

She didn't, of course. Her openness of mind and heart didn't require any fine print. All that she asked for was respect and loyalty. All that she gave in return was unadulterated love and adoration. She was drawn to his life force—that unalterable and mysterious glow inside of each one of us that animates our person in the way the breeze rouses the boughs of the great willow tree to perform *commedia dell'arte*; the invisible ventriloquist of sentience. She felt that our young man's *élan vital* shone as magnificently and promisingly as the crimson sunrise when it offsets an otherwise dark and gloomy world, staving off the forces of evil with an immutable battering ram of heavenly brilliance for yet another day. Had he been honest with her about the anger he harboured up until the moment of their chance encounter, she'd have remained undeterred, so intuitively and immovably confident was she in the goodness that composed the fabric of his being. For, as is so often the case, it is those who love and believe in us who also see and activate the strengths we fail to see in ourselves. It is they who help us remove the blindfold of insecurity that has been preventing us from seeing how truly special we are and can become.

As chance would have it, the pair were also likeminded in their fixation with Homo sapiens' predisposition toward self-sabotage; they were birds of a feather in this obsessive preoccupation. Now cohabitating in an unofficial capacity, their intellectual intercourse, when not interrupted by the physical variety, would often stretch all the way from the bleary-eyed breakfast table by morning to the droopy-eyed pillowcase by night. Their highly engrossed conversations, whether they took the form of heated debate or congruous accord, ebbed and flowed in accordance with the tides.

That they saw eye-to-eye on the macroscopic threats facing humanity wasn't altogether surprising given the context of their era. Once easily dismissed as alarmist and extreme, views such as theirs had become increasingly mainstream with the passage of time and all that it unveiled. For decades, people in growing numbers spanning the array of cultures had developed a clearer and more sobering understanding of the consequences of their own species' actions. As irrefutable evidence piled in mountainous heaps, shadows of doubt were forced to recede like vampires scurrying into the shadows at daybreak. Books enough to fill entire libraries covered the threats humanity posed itself from every imaginable angle. Social movements, some reaching great swells of support, had come and gone to varying degrees of short-lived success. Political will, provided it served the needs of its alter ego, political expedience, had proposed grand visions that either never fully materialized or were scrapped altogether by successive governments pandering to the Achilles' heel of all modern human societies: greed. (It would be unfair here to omit the fact that most governments spared no expense when it came to lip service.) Scientific innovation had boasted time and again of the next great hope, only to fall short of its promise. In their daily lives, individuals reduced, reused, unplugged, renewed, and adopted a litany of other habits to do their part and allay their consciences, but only ever followed through insofar as these practices didn't jeopardize their treasured creature comforts, conveniences that, over time, had become mistaken for necessities like air, food, and water.

Knowing his beloved shared his beliefs caused our young man to stand what felt like a full foot taller. For, is it not the case that we become emboldened when our closest confidants and allies validate our private philosophies, especially when they do so with a sincerity of belief and active interest, not simply because they believe their role to be that of unctuous sycophant?

Now that the fire inside of him roared from a source of love and positivity, he was freed from all impurities of purpose, enabling him to, at long last, stand selflessly before the mighty heavens and raise his staff, free hand over heart, as a solemn and humble declaration of servitude to *life*. No longer possessed by the arrogant and perverted notion that he, out of billions upon billions of his predecessors and contemporaries, had been handpicked to carry out a sick and twisted messianic purpose, our young man joined his sweetheart in dedicating their lives to trying to make the world a better place through positive means, no matter how small the degree of significance; he saw himself as a David rather than a Goliath, and perhaps that's what would make him mightier in the end.

Of all the lessons our young man learned through his newfound humility, the value of listening proved to be the strongest, by a country mile. The world, as it turned out, didn't revolve around him. Turning down the volume on the longwinded, pontificating voice in his head, he began lending his ears to his loving significant other for long and frequent intervals, expanding his knowledge and perspective leaps and bounds in the process, including the discovery of what his own words tasted like. He learned that as with medicine, he must occasionally stomach repugnant flavours to improve his overall wellbeing.

Initially, it must be confessed, his motivation for being so sponge-like in her presence was primarily out of self-interest. Not only did listening keep his foot out of his mouth in the early days of their relationship when the slightest, most minuscule potential misstep was magnified in his mind to the size of a deal-breaker, it was also the best means of conveying his captivated interest. And while he was genuinely interested in her deepest thoughts and feelings, the fear of losing her dictated his behaviour. He felt the need to *act* like someone who was paying attention as much as he actually *was*. Consequently, his head nods, facial expressions, and reactions were noticeably exaggerated. Completely comfortable in her own skin, our young lady found this all very amusing.

But the longer they stayed together and the more confident he became in the strength of their bond, the more relieved was our young man of his deep-seated fear of abandonment. That's not to say that he was able to shed it completely, but what was once a crippling psychological hang-up had faded into the distant background. He eventually became free to be wholly present in her company without constraint or distraction. He was *all hers* without any longer worrying whether she was and would remain *all his*. It was at this point that their souls fused.

For hours that felt like moments to our young man, our young lady would wax on philosophically, taking special care with each chosen word, the better to maintain the integrity and accuracy of the meaning she wished to express. Instead of castigating and condemning her own species as our young man had developed such a negative habit of doing, she analyzed and assessed the threats facing mankind through the empirical and objective lens of a natural scientist. He would hang on her every word, his head resting in his hands, wholly absorbed in adoration.

She would often go into detail about how the fracturing of traditional networks of physical community was preventing the cohesion required to fix the large-scale messes humans had got themselves into. This was because humans shortsightedly placed blind faith in the technological imperative. Their focus was myopic: innovate today, ask questions later. And so they continuously churned out newer and better technologies with the aim of making life as easy as possible, without giving the slightest consideration to the long-term ramifications of their actions. Over time, gadgets had taken priority over relationships. And now, people were spending far more time with their devices than they were with each other.

Examples of this were not in short supply. Who, she'd often ask in rhetorical reflection, could have possibly foreseen the evolution of the telephone? A widely celebrated, historic innovation with the power to contract time and space by uniting two individuals located in different locations and even on opposite shores of an ocean, the telephone boasted of the magical ability to shrink the earth to the size of a baseball by placing access to its many inhabitants in the palm of a hand. Long distance relationships, sons and daughters at war, and various other circumstances that necessitated prolonged separation became increasingly bearable thanks to Alexander Graham Bell and the chain reaction of innovation the telephone had set off. The jury of consumers was unanimous: the telephone was an invention that was of unequivocal benefit to humanity, signaling the dawn of a new paradigm. It would make the world a better place by introducing instant interconnectedness on a global scale. What could possibly go wrong?

She went on to describe how, once the telephone became mobile and made Internet access ubiquitous, everything changed. Rather than just facilitating occasional remote conversations in cases where face-to-face interaction was not possible, cell phones slowly and insidiously became the sole interface through which people felt comfortable interacting with the world around them. Two acquaintances sitting in the same room were more likely to engage with those located elsewhere than they were each other. The phone became a bona fide extension of the human body, a portable wormhole to anywhere other than where one was. It was for this reason that people who lost or broke their phones became panic-stricken and deeply aggrieved; it was as if they had fractured or severed a limb. To many, the sense of pain and loss was as great, if not greater.

With a virtual universe now available to human beings on demand, she continued, people the world over immersed and lost themselves in digital worlds of their own creation. They chose artificial representations of self over the real thing because it provided the choices Mother Nature, ever the stingy and strict maternal guardian, did not. None were forced to any longer try and love themselves for who they really were. Anyone could now be, or at least feel and create the impression they were, precisely who they wanted to be, even if it were only in avataristic form. Authenticity had completely given way to superficiality. Appearances became everything. Fat could appear thin. Lonely could appear popular. Poor could appear rich. Boring could appear exciting. And with everyone plugged into the same substitute dimension, how they depicted themselves on the Internet became all that mattered. Surreality had become the new reality. The online world supplanted religion as the modern-day opiate for the masses. When given the option to follow God or become one, was there ever any doubt about the choice humans would make, and the direction things would take?

Moreover, our young lady never failed to point out, all had a platform upon which to declare their boasts, woes, political bents, and other self-important opinions and philosophies to the entire globe (or so they felt). Millions of people spent tremendous amounts of time and energy advertising and promoting their personal brands in a relentless and, more often than not, doomed effort to move up the virtual social ladder and develop a literal following of worshippers. Everyone, without exception, could suddenly aspire to icon status. All they had to sacrifice was a more meaningful and natural experience of life—a small price to pay for the chance to one day be celebrated and fawned over. To be heard. To be thought of. To be adored. To be remembered. To feel and perhaps even become… immortal.

With everyone vying for individual attention and narcissistic supremacy, the struggle to be noticed became a scene of pack animals fighting over the carcass of their prey, pulling, tearing, and gnashing at as much of the remaining flesh as they could sink their fangs into. Naturally—or unnaturally—increasingly extreme measures were taken to stand out from the crowd. To be noticed by others, most of whom were complete strangers, became life's primary pursuit and goal. Whatever it took.

The consequences of all this obsessive reliance on technology, she continued as the weeks and months blurred together, was the dilution and disintegration of traditional human bonds. All were polar bears drifting away on shrinking chunks of ice, distracted from their common plight by the hollow reflection of their own sallow faces in the melting arctic waters. The self had become the centre of the universe around which everything else revolved.

Then one day, without warning, our young lady decided she was through with talking. Together, they had saved the planet, uplifted the less fortunate, and curbed Artificial Intelligence thousands of times in their minds. If ever they were to make a real difference, they couldn't go on daydreaming forever. It was time for action. It was time to be bold and take a proactive first step toward making manifest their shared sense of purpose.

Riding this gust of motivation, our young woman sat our young man down to discuss the plan she had devised. She decided that it was time the two of them set sail into the big, intimidating world via that great vessel of opportunity—University. Although there was no guarantee they would reach their charted destination, University offered unmatched exposure to a broad spectrum of people and opportunities. It was a good place to start.

Although he agreed and played along outwardly, our young man wasn't sure this was really the direction in which he wanted their relationship to head. Deep down, he had begun to yearn for a simple and unassuming life together. He had money enough to take care of them both. They didn't need to go to school. The more she got to see what the world had to offer, he feared, the more exposed he would be for how underwhelming he truly was. He wanted her all to himself, and was deathly afraid of losing her. Consequently, he viewed the doors to University and all they represented as an ominous threat.

Ultimately, however, his neurotic fear of losing her outweighed his neurotic jealousy by a wide margin. He was left with no choice but to hide his insecurity and face his fears head on. University it would be. How would it all unfold? Only time would tell.

O time, you most precious and scarce commodity; thou who giveth and taketh away hope. While we may find ourselves wishing you away, we could always use more of you. We watch the grains fall through an hourglass firmly affixed to the table; can't it be flipped over to give us just a little more, please? The hands on a clock may be reversed or even snapped off, for that matter, but your persistence transcends all that which represents you; none can be as reliable. We are obsessed with you precisely because we die, and of that, you are a constant reminder. We ask about you incessantly; check in at regular intervals to determine how much of you has slipped away. We use you up reminiscing of remembrances you'll never give us back. And if that weren't cruel enough, our experience of you accelerates as we age, and perception is real to those perceiving it; each of us discovers relativity independently; as we stand on the platform of life, the train leaves the station no sooner than it arrives; and for better or for worse, we move unceasingly toward our end.

Of all life's many and diverse experiences, there is one that brings the tireless march of time to the fore of the conscious self more than any other. Unlike time itself, this experience is completely disorderly and unpredictable; it is the structural antithesis of time. It is, however, as has already been pointed out, the one experience in life that causes us to clutch hopelessly at something completely and forever out of our control, as if it were thin air, because it has made us realize how much we truly wish to breathe for multiple eternities, only to remind ourselves how unlikely it is to breathe for a meager century, and it is an agonizing drawback from the enjoyment of happiness to remind ourselves that it cannot last; which is why the experience that makes us most aware of our own existential limits is also the experience that makes us happiest, or saddest should it elude our attainment. That experience, of course, is love. Therefore, O time, in the name of love, can we not have a little more time?

VI

Higher education. For many who enroll, a more fitting double entendre cannot exist. After an upbringing characterized by the constant oversight and coddling of caregivers, the primary allure of college and university for these students is finally having the freedom to do what they want. This generally means overcompensating years of deprivation with excess. Whether they've enrolled in an economics program or not, most who leave home for the first time quickly figure out the formula to the most important and pressing question of all: what canned slop or gruel can they survive on to ensure they've enough purchase power remaining to keep their chosen vices readily available? (Parents, if alcohol is your sole concern, consider yourself lucky… or naïve… or both.) It may be tattered and missing a significant number of pages, but the discount for buying a used textbook means there'll be enough left over to invest in a debilitating hangover.

For students who somehow manage to stay on track academically, University is also a time to tap into something more profound than a keg: the mind. It is where one is encouraged to bore beneath the superficial, everyday layers of cognition into the cavernous domain of the philosophical, where future luminaries uncover their hidden phosphorescence. It is there, in the imagination's abyss, where curious and maturing thinkers travel to explore the more weighty and unanswerable of life's questions in hopes of making sense of a world and universe that no longer seems as orderly and safe as it did in the comforts of their family home or the smaller communities of their upbringing. It is at University where worldviews that have only ever been reinforced and validated by like minds who share beliefs and espouse them as maxims are challenged by new and differing perspectives and secularism, that old, pesky inconvenience to dogmatic thinking. Biases like bigoted and sexist tendencies, however innocent their intent may claim to be, will be met by fierce resistance, so wise students learn quickly to either purge them altogether or keep such biases to themselves, as they are no longer Universal in the definitive sense. Vast horizons of thought are opened for exploration. Empiricism is encouraged. Theodicy is replaced by scientific explanation and verification. Perhaps that fatal heart attack wasn't a direct punishment for adultery, after all. Physiology says otherwise. Begone, myth and superstition—evidence has taken your place here on campus. The real test to determine the difference between right and wrong is open and subject to endless debate; morality is frustratingly untethered. Irrespective of the lenses through which we make sense of the world around us, we engage in deeper and more reflective thought, for better or for worse, for good and for evil. Self-importance is challenged. The insignificance of life is made abundantly clear.

These are but a few of the true lessons we are taught at University. In theory, at least.

Our young couple, by contrast, didn't fit either scenario. They were by then old souls whose wisdom had leapfrogged their years and then some. Both were already far along the path of discovering what their minds were capable of; they had struck out along that journey some time ago. They had by then, as autodidacts with inquisitiveness to spare, traversed vast mountain ranges and sailed expansive seas of higher order thinking. No ordinary freshmen, they were PhDs without letters, unbridled scholarly thoroughbreds. Finding themselves in a unique financial situation where both had access to a significant amount of wealth that had been bequeathed to them, future earning potential was not on their minds or even on their radar. They had enrolled in University for one purpose and one purpose only: as a point-of-entry into the *system* so they could do what they had to do and meet who they needed to meet to climb the ladders that had to be climbed to gain the credibility they needed to devote their lives toward doing their part to help to rescue their species from itself.

Is it not the case that when we put our minds to something with pure and good intentions, doors begin to open and things start to happen in our favour? That if our motivations come from a genuine place, fate tends to take our side? While the answers to these questions can never be proven in any definitive sense, few would disagree with the assertion that positive thinking manifests itself as positive outcomes.

And so it would be for our young, amorous scholars. In just their first few months living on campus, while they were still in the process of adjusting to their new surroundings and routine, a chance encounter would forever change their lives. It took place while they were traversing the well-manicured outdoor common grounds in search of a lecture hall where an extracurricular meeting they wished to attend was being held. In stark contrast to the cracked and thirsty soil that typified the University's neighbouring communities, this was a vibrant green lawn framed by symmetrical rows of old growth trees, producing an idyllic setting for students to sprawl out and soak in both daylight and knowledge. Unfamiliar with where they were headed and short on time, our young couple approached a rather peculiar-looking character to ask for directions.

Ambiguously gendered by all outward appearances, this individual sat languidly in the mold of Alice's caterpillar, drawing in and exhaling gigantic plumes from a modern sort of hookah pipe. Hair, dyed most every colour of the rainbow, sprang jagged and shaggy like that of an anime hero, with bangs covering just enough of their eyes to render them expressionless and inscrutable. Nose, face, and mouth were studded with piercings, skin blanketed with body art. They wore sleek, form-fitting pants and elven shoes curled up at the toes. *Activist* was written all over them.

As might be expected from such outwardly radical and rebellious figures, our young couple were met with a chilly reception, to say the least. Emitting the hostility of a guerrilla fighter with no time for civilian matters, the Activist, without so much as tilting their glance upwards to see who was addressing them, raised a lean and muscled arm and silently pointed in response to our young couple's directional query. Like an insurgent wholly focused on assembling a gun for an impending battle, this Activist remained absorbed in the pages of a book.

Squinting to read the title on the cover, our young lady recognized the book as one she had already read. It was a non-fiction that sounded the alarm about Artificial Intelligence and its slow and insidious quest to syphon the secrets of the human brain and render Homo sapiens dependent upon and consequently subservient to a machine of their own making. Its central tenet held that the unquenchable human desire for greater and greater convenience eventually backfired into the unwitting renunciation of autonomy from and control over the monster it had created. Technology had evolved into a formidable enemy. Frankenstein's creature was real.

Although she knew she'd irritate the Activist by further breaching their privacy barrier, our young lady couldn't help but volunteer her unsolicited critique of the book. She opined that, while she felt the book helped spread broad awareness about a major threat facing society, it was far too esoteric and catastrophic to resonate with a general audience. The technical stuff was too technical, and the message was too gloomy for everyday readers. She then recommended another, newer book that she felt did a much better job of helping people comprehend the day-to-day symptoms and consequences of Artificial Intelligence's tightening grip on the human brain; it was accessible and balanced without pulling any punches.

As if what she had said were the missing "Abracadabra!" and "Open sesame!" required to gain access beyond what, by all outward appearances, was an impenetrable forcefield, the Activist slowly marked the page, closed the book, and lifted their gaze to meet the eyes of our young lady and her male companion. Like a business executive who just discovered that the people they had been disregarding could be useful, the Activist had, from one moment to the next, switched from complete indifference to granting their undivided attention. For proudly irreverent and disestablishmentarian souls such as this, granting seemingly average people the time of day is a rare privilege indeed.

Curiosity piqued and interest caught, the Activist stood up, brushed the brush from the seat of their pants, and introduced themself using a moniker that, in addition to being less believable as a given name than that of an exotic dancer, did nothing to shed light on their gender.

Introductions having been made, the Activist offered to accompany our young lovers to the location of the lecture hall about which they had initially inquired. Seeing no good reason to object, our young couple, after silently conferring with one another by way of a quick side glance, acquiesced with nods and shrugs in the affirmative. And, like that, the three of them were off, two newbies and their unofficial on-campus guide, strolling together along a plush and vibrant terrain located somewhere on the vast and increasingly barren planet.

Along the way, our young lady and the Activist wasted no time diving right into conversation about the threat posed by AI. Our young lady would never pass up the opportunity to discuss, debate, and advocate for her beliefs. To her, Artificial Intelligence was the most pressing matter of the day and was, therefore, always worth talking about. To change one person was to change the world. The Activist, on the other hand, listened intently as if quietly testing her to find out how knowledgeable she really was on the topic. Both were immediately and completely engrossed.

While our young lady and the Activist were so embroiled, our young man, keeping stride in body, receded in mind. As he withdrew, he thought longingly of his mother, yet felt a sense of fulfillment he hadn't experienced since he was a toddler. The void left by her passing had finally been filled after all these years by the young woman with whom he had established an exclusive romantic bond. He had her all to himself and it was wonderful. She had, in some bizarre surrogate way, reconnected our young man with the emotional safety associated with the earliest remembrances of his upbringing. Precisely as it had been, it was to be again. His *raison d'être* was a woman who loved him without condition.

Awakened from this daydream by the sound of our young lady's voice waxing on with the same conviction and mastery of one of history's great orators, our young man returned to the present with a passive grin etched onto his face. He was happy, plain and simple. Perhaps all the pain and suffering he had endured hadn't been a curse after all. Perhaps it had all simply been a series of challenges laid before him to determine his worthiness to win the hand of an angel sent to earth to help rescue it; a demi-god dispatched by the twelve Olympians to rescue the mortal world from its own shortcomings. While it was a silly and far-fetched thought, he couldn't help but place her on a pedestal. He genuinely believed she would one day make good on her altruistic ambitions and leave her stamp on history. She was, in his eyes, a young, modern-day Joan of Arc in the making.

His mind had drifted yet again. As their destination finally came into view, our young man solemnly swore to himself that he would never let anything happen to her so long as his heart continued to pump blood through his veins. It pained him to think where he'd be without her. He would love and protect her to the grave.

After arriving at the front steps of the building where they were scheduled to be in a few minutes' time, our young couple thanked the Activist. Without offering so much as a word in reply, the Activist removed a pen and old scrap of paper from their ragged bag and began to jot something down using their thigh as a makeshift desk. Confused, our young couple awkwardly waited.

Just as the couple began reminding each other that they had better get going, the Activist, after looking over both shoulders to determine whether anyone else was watching or within earshot, leaned in and secretively handed our young woman the paper. The handoff thus complete, the Activist coyly conveyed that they felt confident our young couple could be trusted, and, without elaborating, strode away briskly into the distance, lacking only cape, sabre, and steed to complete the dramatic exit.

Once the Activist was out of view, our young couple huddled close together to examine what it was they had been handed. It was... the map of an unfamiliar intersection.

Below the map was a designated date and time. There was no further information. After a quick online search, they learned that it was a map to what looked to be an abandoned concrete wasteland a way away.

The bell from the building rang to indicate the hour. They were late. In haste, they burst through the front doors in the same manner as countless tardy students have dating back to the era of one-room schoolhouses.

VII

Standing at an actual crossroads located in an uninhabited industrial village on the distant outskirts of town, our young lovers began to question their decision to follow a makeshift map they'd been handed by a stranger. Were they correct in their interpretation that the noted time meant morning? Would they bother going back later that day had they been wrong? Moreover, they had no idea what they were being invited to or why they were being invited. Their best guess was that it had something to do with what the Activist and our young woman had been discussing, but there was no way to be sure. Their surroundings were completely deserted. An unsettling feeling set in. Had they naively placed themselves in grave danger?

Like the cat, curiosity can kill our ability to make responsible decisions, causing us to willingly and predictably roll the dice on the unknown and exciting rather than simply turning it down in the name of prudence. Like a phantom temptress, curiosity lures us into the mists of tantalizing mystery, disabling our ability to foresee consequences, and setting the stage for the very real possibility of regret. The thrill of taking a risk hypnotizes us into following our curiosity into the unknown against our better judgment. What good is human sagacity when it abandons us at times when we need it the most?

And so it was with our young couple as they stood in the middle of a sweltering cement wasteland, questioning why they had come and what they were waiting for, if anything at all. Doubts and alarm bells filled their brains, yet they resisted the primal urge to flee. Had he not felt the need to prove his courage, our young man wouldn't have agreed to go in the first place. The more time passed, the more he lost his nerve. She, by contrast, remained outwardly unflappable. He tried his best to keep up a brave face, but his paranoia mounted. With perspiration accumulating on his palms, he eventually caved and suggested they should probably leave. The appointed time had passed by some minutes, and the time to depart had arrived. He had a bad feeling about this. After taking a moment to consider the matter, she begrudgingly acquiesced. They would head back.

Just as they took their first few paces toward the closest public transit terminal (located no short walk away), the hands of fate, akin to the white-gloved hands of a magician with a flair for the dramatic, went to work. On the shimmering horizon, our young man spotted a tinted and menacing-looking black vehicle rumbling in their direction at an alarming speed. As he stood frozen with a gaping mouth, our young lady grabbed him by the wrist and led him hurriedly in the opposite direction. He didn't need any convincing.

No sooner had they broken into a run than they spotted a second vehicle of the exact same make and model round a corner and accelerate toward them. Hemmed in north and south, they glanced east and west in search of a possible escape route. To their mounting despair, they discovered they were being pursued from all sides. There was nowhere to run. All feeling drained from our young man's legs.

After a quick scan of their getaway options, our composed and quick-thinking young lady located a door that was open no more than a crack along the side of a condemned building not far from where they stood. She motioned to our young man to follow her lead, and the pair took flight with the alacrity of anyone who's ever run for their life.

Bursting through the door and slamming it closed behind them, they piled some unidentifiable and rather heavy ballast they found by the entranceway against the inside of the door to barricade it shut and buy some precious time. Their chests heaved with breathlessness. Their hearts pounded with adrenaline.

After weaving their way through multiple rows of large and dust-covered commercial equipment, they stumbled upon a large opening. Their eyes had by then adjusted to their dimly lit surroundings. They found themselves in what, by all appearances, was the storage area of a former abattoir or meat packaging facility. Even in their distressed state, they didn't fail to recognize the dark humour in the situation—they had entered a slaughterhouse.

As they ventured deeper into perilous uncertainty, they observed evidence of Mother Nature reclaiming what had once been Hers. The concrete laid long ago to suffocate any and all plant life beneath it was discovering the truly resilient and irrepressible essential thrust of life. Weeds and shrubs had erupted through cracks in the floor. Sprawling vines spread their tendrils across the walls. A dusty ray of light cast a spotlight on the intricacies of an abandoned bird's nest. On some level, nature's resilience buoyed our young couple's spirits; life's indefatigable determination boosted their own will to live. Something primeval was compelling them onward, like a whisper that can only be understood without being heard.

But Mother Nature wasn't their only company. Noises in the background indicated that their pursuers had breached their blockade and were hot on their trail. To make matters worse, it became increasingly difficult to see as they ventured deeper into the intensifying darkness. They soon lost track of their direction and couldn't light their way for fear of giving up their position.

Fearful of bumping into something and making a sound, our young couple crouched into a small nook hidden behind a large metallic contraption. The sound of their pulses thudded loudly in their temples. Calling upon every ounce of self-control they could muster, they remained perfectly silent and still.

Refusing to play the role of sitting duck, our young woman discreetly removed her mobile communication device to alert the authorities of their whereabouts and that they were in immediate danger. Much to her gut-wrenching dismay, the signal had been scrambled in the building.

Our young man checked his mobile phone, but it had been scrambled, too. He dejectedly lowered his head. The sound of approaching footsteps and shuffling bodies grew nearer. Time was running out.

As was his habit, our terrified young man became swallowed by his own thoughts. There, somewhere in his inner universe, he had a flashback to the sound of footsteps approaching his childhood home mere moments before his mother had been mercilessly slaughtered. He had always envisioned that the emotional scarring from that memory would thicken his skin and bring him great strength and valour if ever a similar situation presented itself. How wrong he had been! He was no less terrified and helpless at that moment than his younger self had been the first time around. But this time, he was a grown man with a life partner to protect, making his debilitating fear seem even more self-castrating. How could he possibly still be so spineless? For the first time in his life, our self-proclaimed young atheist began to pray.

Flashlight beams came into view above the machinery behind which they hid. Harbingers of the approaching search party, they were a cluster of moons dancing on a cosmic backdrop. To the startled astonishment of our young man, our young lady called out in a confident voice, demanding to know who their pursuers were and what they wanted.

The footsteps halted. A calm and collected voice responded with reassurances that our young couple wasn't in any danger. This was simply a precaution they would come to understand in time. They were safe. They had his word. The unfamiliar male voice then asked that they please move out into the open with their hands above their heads.

Not buying it, our young lady probed further, requiring more than empty assurances. Where was the Activist who had invited them there? What did they want? How could they trust they wouldn't be harmed?

There was no reply. The march of footsteps resumed.

It was at this point that our intrepid young lady whispered to our young man that they were going to have to make a run for it. He was to follow her lead and not look back. After he acknowledged that he understood the plan, she began counting down from three. As she did so, a beam of a light swept across the wall not far from our young man's head, causing him to gasp audibly. His faintheartedness had given them up.

They were cornered. The brightness of the flashlights was blinding in contrast to the surrounding darkness. Our young lady stood up to face whatever it was fate had in store for her with fearless dignity. Her squinting eyes glared right back at the firearms staring her down. Looking weak and pathetic by comparison, our young man slowly got to his feet and slunk behind her. Out of options, the pair raised their arms in surrender.

VIII

After having been blindfolded, transported in the back of a vehicle for what felt like the better part of an eternity, and marched with their hands bound behind their backs into an unknown building, our young couple had understandably begun to expect the worst. They could tell they had been shuttled indoors by a sudden shift in background noise from the chirrups of nature to the whirl of fans and din of electronics. They were smart enough to accept that struggling was futile and would only serve to make matters worse. They wanted desperately to whisper their undying love to another, lest they never have the chance again, but held their tongues in the event that, by cooperating with their captors, they did.

While in this state of mind, their blindfolds were removed to reveal the furthest thing from what either of them could have envisioned in their wildest imagination. Standing directly before them was the Activist, dressed as radically as their first encounter, only grinning on this occasion with the warmth and sincerity of a gracious host welcoming distinguished guests to join them at the hearth. Behind the Activist lay a sprawling network of computers and communications technology that lit up and flickered like the electrical grid of a metropolis as viewed from an airplane at night. At regular intervals, people dressed in nondescript leisurewear sat at workstations, toiling away without so much as lifting their eyes to take note of their visitors. Their desks were oddly bare. Whatever it was they were working on, they were laser focused.

Before our young couple had a chance to inquire as to the meaning of it all, the Activist began by apologizing profusely for having to kidnap them, stressing that it was out of absolute necessity to protect the secrecy of their whereabouts. Because people don't generally respond well to invitations that require being blindfolded and transported to a mysterious location for reasons unknown, the abduction was, regrettably, mandatory. They were safe and at liberty to move about and speak freely, including any questions they might have.

The restraints were then removed from our young couple's wrists.

It was at this point that our young lady rushed upon the Activist, pinning them to the wall by the collar and forcefully demanding an explanation. Everyone within earshot, including our young man, looked on in disbelief.

Before the abductors tending to our young couple could intervene, the Activist, veins bulging from their forehead and gasping for air, raised a hand to call them off. Straining to get the words out, the Activist swore to our young lady—as if she, vastly outnumbered, were nevertheless in control—that she would get her explanation. Assuaged, our young lady released the Activist from her clutch and stepped back.

Tensions eased, the Activist broke into an explanatory monologue.

What our young couple saw before them was the headquarters of a network of the country's most gifted and experienced hackers, many of whom had begun their careers as digital outlaws and rogues, but had since defected to the side of Good. Together, they formed a budding rebel group that had been assembled over the course of many months. Rigorous precautions had had to be taken to scout and vet new recruits, all while evading public detection. Beyond those walls, not a soul knew about their existence. They were ghosts operating entirely off the grid. Their homemade energy source was renewable and untraceable. They had assembled the collective brainpower to cause the global economy to collapse. They had the ability to obtain and spend as much money as they wanted, any time they needed it, without leaving so much as a breadcrumb in their wake. They were also armed in case they were ever discovered and forced to defend themselves. One of their core guiding principles, however, was to first exhaust all options to achieve their aims without resorting to the use of violence. To be meticulous and vigilant was their mantra.

The iron grip of fear having by then loosened from his chest, our young man, overflowing with insecurity and shame stemming from his string of shortcomings in the area of valiance, failed to suppress an impulsive and foolhardy outburst. Puffing out his chest in a physical display of overcompensation, he demanded they be freed that instant—or else. Who did they think they were, taking people hostage against their will? They were nothing more than thugs masquerading as vigilantes. They would pay for this! Even as he made the pointless threat, he knew it was a cringeworthy display.

Never without a keen instinct for what the moment required, our young lady placed her hand gently on our young man's shoulder as a means of diffusing his anger without causing the slightest offence. Deeply embarrassed with himself, our young man went quiet, crossed his arms, and lowered his furrowed brow.

Like a parent waiting for a tantrum to run its course, the Activist paused composedly to ensure our young man was done before resuming.

The abduction of our young couple, explained the Activist, was all part of a recruitment initiative of great importance and urgency. In our young lady, the Activist saw the elusive leader the rebels so desperately needed and had long been searching for. The day of their chance encounter on campus, the eloquence and command with which our young lady described the clear and present danger the Internet posed human society left a lasting impression on the Activist. Without fear of reprisal and with unfaltering confidence, she made a compelling and airtight case to a stranger that the online world was the most powerful drug humans had ever invented. It was more addictive and readily available than all known narcotics combined, she had argued. The next fix was always right there at one's fingertips. An addict *might* avert their eyes from the screen to avoid bumping into a passerby or walking into traffic, but they would return to their digital escape at their next given opportunity as sure as the day they were born.

The natural consequence, our young lady had so astutely observed, was that human thought atrophied into a giant heap of mush. Most could no longer pay attention to anything for more than a minute or so at a time, and even that was pushing it. All manner of people had become entirely dependent. They still had access to all the information they required, so nothing seemed different on the surface, but they no longer stored it on the shelves of their own brains. Information was being extracted and housed by a third party, where it could be accessed anytime, but for a price. People of all ages were leaking knowledge in vast quantities. The Internet was thinking for them. Master and slave were trading places.

As the Activist waxed on, piecing together what our young lady had said with more passion than cohesion, our young lady couldn't help but feel an overwhelming amount of pride hearing her own worldview repeated back to her. She had invested so much time and energy cultivating and distilling her beliefs over the years. To receive that sort of validation and praise from a high-ranking rebel in front of their comrades was a dream come true. Was it really happening? In a matter of months, she had gone from the brink of despair to finding true love and having her calling answered. After silently thanking her late twin and lucky stars, she squeezed our young man's hand to communicate her joy.

And while our young man was compelled to outwardly pretend he felt the same way, he experienced debilitating insecurity on the inside, hindering his ability to genuinely share in our young woman's excitement. He was witnessing the fulfillment of her dream. He had no right to get in the way. Doing so would only wind up backfiring. He felt he had no choice but to suffer in silence.

In effect, the Activist continued, still paraphrasing our young woman, human beings had sold their faculties—the one advantage they had over all other species in the animal kingdom—to the devil in exchange for the very thoughts they had for so long been able to produce on their own. Playing his greatest trick yet, Lucifer was luring the entire population toward damnation with nothing more than the promise of cheap vanity and sloth. In return, he gained the one thing he needed to drag humanity into the concentric rings of the Inferno—control over their minds.

With direct access to our feelings, motivations, understanding, and personality, the Internet was obtaining the secrets to human sentience for its own purposes. A sinister takeover was underway and gaining momentum. Artificial Intelligence was developing the ability to think for itself. Algorithmic consciousness was only a matter of time; a question of *when*, not *if*. It was an imminent threat to the future of the species, a worst fear coming true, yet the unconditional champions of progress blindly cheered its advancement. One didn't have to look far for evidence of AI's strengthening grip over its master. Skyrocketing unemployment rates and plummeting literacy scores told the story as good as any. Without jobs or skills, human beings were reverting to monosyllabic brutes; manpower was being harnessed and shepherded by the machine. An overthrow was taking place right beneath people's noses.

The effects of long-term Internet use began to weigh heavily and take their toll on society, the Activist continued, as if reciting passages written by a well-known philosopher. And like with any addiction, ailing health wasn't enough to bring about reform. Dependence was such that people would sooner risk an early grave than disconnect. The prevalence of mental illness went from an upward trend worthy of public discussion to a widespread chronic disease in no more than a few short generations. Suicide quickly climbed the ranks of causes of death. So ordinary had it become to take one's own life that parents no longer blamed themselves. Severe mental illness was a widespread pandemic, and addiction to the Internet was the primary underlying cause.

And yet most people continued living in oblivion. Whether it was out of ignorance or willful blindness, their reliance upon the spellbinding glow of screens seemed incurable. Humanity was being conquered by its own devices, as it were, yet people were too self-consumed and apathetic to do anything about it.

But our young lady knew all of this, emphasized the Activist. They were her thoughts. That was why she was there. She had left an indelible impression. That there was something special about her was undeniable. She was the chosen one, born to lead the revolution the rebels would set into motion—the Activist was convinced of it. All that remained was to obtain the assent of the other members of the rebels' senior council.

But they were getting ahead of themselves, the Activist self-interrupted, as one does when recalling something important they've forgotten to mention. Before proceeding any further, the Activist owed our young couple some more background on the rebels and their history:

A few years ago, the founder of their movement, widely considered history's most notorious hacker, had experienced a great epiphany. Like being awakened from a lifetime's hypnosis, this individual came to the eye-opening realization that he had been unwittingly living in the service of a great evil. Up until then, he had derived sick satisfaction from the sense of power he got from wreaking havoc on what he viewed as everyday automatons, mindlessly going about their business like a flock of sheep that was deserving of punishment for their meek and gutless servility to the system.

The unprecedented computational powers he yielded won him the street alias *God*. And just like God, he could destroy lives at random and on a whim without so much as a warning or explanation why. When in a rare agreeable mood, he would grant clemency and spare would-be victims, but never without making clear that he could have snapped their financial or reputational spines like a pencil, had he been inclined.

God's insatiable thirst for absolute power was a form of overcompensation for a profound sense of inadequacy he had acquired over the course of an abusive and impoverished upbringing. His story was all too familiar, but, to him, his struggle was unparalleled. No one could understand and everyone was to blame. Vengeance was their just deserts.

Mastery over the digital universe was his weapon of mass revenge *and* destruction. An automatic rifle, in his eyes, was a slingshot by comparison. Short of the ability to conjure earthquakes and pestilence, this God injected some of the most virulent diseases the world has ever known directly into the veins of the Internet, putting all who surfed its tempestuous seas at risk of exposure. That he was an archvillain was unquestionable. The combination of his anonymity and fame (or infamy) won him legions of cult supporters. People silently cheered his evasiveness. He was a phantom, a hair-raising myth used to scare children into doing their chores.

It wasn't until he fell hopelessly smitten for another man that God's heart finally softened from stone to human tissue, releasing his long-lost vulnerability and humanity from captivity. At the height of their courtship, God, in a private moment, confidentially revealed what it was he did for a living—a decision he had struggled with mightily.

As might be expected, this disclosure was met with severe disapproval. His partner presented him with an ultimatum: reform his ways or they would be parting ways.

And so God, rendered vulnerable by the fear of missing out on love, vowed to change his ways in order to make things work. It was an alcoholic promising their spouse to never touch another drop so long as they lived.

As the craving to inflict pain on others abated, God started to see himself for what he really was with objective clarity. He was a monster, an ambassador of evil. Love awakened God to the fact that he had been nothing more than a spiteful soul forcing everyone else to join him in his misery and suffering.

God also came to the realization that he had never actually been in control of his own destiny, as he'd thought. Far from it. Instead, he had been a patsy aiding the rise of the greatest evil overlord the world would ever know. With each act of terror God had committed, the Internet's neurotransmitters were taking notes and evolving. As the digital universe learned to think for itself, God was playing the part of private tutor, helping it plot the overthrow of mankind. He was lighting the dark path to hell. Each hack, each breach of private and confidential information, was training the Internet how to oppress its maker and achieve supremacy atop the throne of planet earth and perhaps beyond. God created man, man created machines, machines created God, God unwittingly helped machines enslave man.

God was forced to confront the painful truth that his had been the hands prying open the lid to Pandora's box. In the name of love and making amends, he became hell bent on slamming it shut.

Eager to repair all the damage he now realized he had caused, God thought long and hard about how he might apply his powers to reverse it. What people needed was a true redeemer, not to be kicked while they were down. They needed a highly sophisticated rebel organization to lead a virtual crusade to emancipate them from their captivity, to awaken them from their hegemonic stupor and inspire them to revolt against their omniscient oppressor. There had been sizeable waves of resistance and protest over the years, but nothing approaching the large-scale coordination and participation required to stave off an impending apocalypse. God decided that he would live up to his name and take on the responsibility of saviour. From that day forward, he vowed to right his wrongs and lead the charge against the mounting threat of AI.

God's first order of business was to conscript the services of his peers from the underbelly of online terrorism. His hope was that his status as the best to ever do it would help lure his contemporaries into agreeing to become his associates. In the esteem of the hacking community, there was God, and then there was everyone else. And so God, confident in his status and influence, put out an encrypted call on the dark web to enlist other legendary hackers to join him.

Unfortunately for God, his plan didn't initially turn out the way he had intended. Like a gang member that defected from a sworn criminal's lifestyle, all that God accomplished by announcing his plans was to have a bounty placed on his own head. Those who had received his invitation were highly suspicious of it. Was God now working for the authorities? Had he been compromised and was now planning to entrap them as part of a plea agreement? Consequently, all God received in return for his recruitment efforts were threats against his life.

Undeterred, God decided to go it alone. Such was his belief in his own abilities. This newly benevolent, born again God spared no time getting down to work. The road ahead was as long as it was uncertain and perilous, but perhaps his example would be enough to spark a passion in others to follow in his footsteps. He had to try.

But for months that felt like centuries, God spun his wheels and got nowhere. Perhaps God the all-powerful had finally bitten off more than he could chew. Not even he could take on this crusade alone. Doubt, a foreign feeling for someone so mighty, began to creep in. Perhaps it was time to throw in the towel and accept defeat.

With hope teetering on its last leg, God received an unexpected encrypted message from a precocious young hacker he had never heard of. In the note, the young hacker praised God's efforts, articulated profound admiration for his work, and espoused an aspiration to one day work alongside him in the capacity of acolyte.

Aware of the possibility that it was a trick, but equally excited at the prospect of reviving his vision, God arranged to meet with this individual in private. Trusting his instincts proved to be a sage move. That individual turned out to be the Activist. The rebel movement was now two strong.

Over time, as more pieces began to fall into place, the number of new recruits grew. Once a nucleus was formed, a governance structure and constitution were established, including provisions to safeguard the secrecy of the movement and protect the identities of the rebels. Each new recruit signed their life over to the movement. All the momentum seemed to be in their favour.

Sadly, it wasn't to be in the end. God was being investigated by a counter-cyberterrorism unit at the same time. During their investigation, they tracked down several petty hackers and roughed them up for information about what they knew. More than willing to cough up any goods they had to save their own necks, these wannabes didn't hesitate to spill any and all the beans at their disposal.

With the fervor of an investigation bureau systematically dismantling a racketeering ring, the authorities eventually closed in on the newly formed rebels and shook them down one by one. Out of self-preservation, one or two of the weakest-willed among them cracked and sacrificed God to save themselves.

Late one night, as God lay intimately with his boyfriend on the couch, a SWAT team ambushed their apartment and killed them both without warning. The authorities framed the scene to make it seem like God's partner had committed a crime of passion before turning the gun on himself. The media printed exactly what the police fed them, but unnoticed nearby witnesses helped to ensure the truth survived through word of mouth. Conspiracy theories abounded.

Their leader dead and their lives now in danger by association, the newly formed rebels disbanded, retreating into the dark recesses like roaches scurrying into baseboards when a light is switched on. Just as their movement was taking flight, it had been run aground and torn asunder.

But the embers of God's legacy were never fully extinguished. His true, core disciples refused to abandon his vision and legacy, even at the risk of grave danger. As a martyr, God became far more powerful than when he was mortal flesh and blood. His words became sacred. Like specters leaping from shadow to shadow, a small group of loyalists maintained contact with one another while lying dormant, patiently plotting their resurgence from the sidelines. After a long period of exile, the seeds that survived the winter of the rebels' dissolution began to germinate anew.

To evade detection, the surviving hackers used fake identities to purchase an abandoned building under the pretext of starting a business. To avoid suspicion, they obeyed every single conceivable government requirement on time and to the letter. Proof of purchase, articles of incorporation, tax returns, and comprehensive audit trails all appeared magically alongside legitimate businesses in official government records. By all outward appearances, the rebels were model business owners operating a moderately successful online company that employed a solid number of tax-paying citizens. Officials never gave them a second look. It was all quite impressive, really.

Sheltered from the scrutinizing eyes of the state in their newly acquired home base, the rebels built from scratch a central hub or headquarters that was neither reliant upon nor discoverable by the grid connecting the outside world. Powered by the elements and cloaked in homemade masking technology, the newly revived rebels created an untraceable operation, carving out the sanctuary required to prepare for an impending existential war.

But they needed a leader. One of the things that had quickly become apparent was that, for all they had established in a short span, the rebels remained a motley and disorganized bunch of strong-minded outsiders. These were antisocial, reclusive personalities. It would be unreasonable to expect them to spontaneously transform into cooperative social beings in the absence of a unifying commander. Not surprisingly, ego clashes were happening at every turn. In group situations, disagreements frequently escalated into tense conflict that required the intervention of others. It was like trying to join two magnets at the same pole; the closer they were forced to be to one another, the more repulsion they exhibited.

In God's successor, the rebels needed a persuasive and authoritative personality with the wisdom, conviction, and clarity of vision to set them on a path toward a common goal; someone whose nature it was to inspire and cultivate solidarity; someone to look up to and believe in.

During their chance encounter that day on campus, the Activist became convinced beyond dissuasion that our young lady was that very person. A devout nihilist, the Activist believed that God had orchestrated their meeting from beyond the grave. It was a sign. Of all the places on earth, both were meant to be in the same place at the same time. Their encounter was no random occurrence; it had been ordained by God. She was the chosen one.

As the longest serving rebel, the Activist was certain they had found their elusive leader. But one vote alone was not enough to grant the chief appointment. As previously mentioned, a quorum would have to be reached among the rebels' senior council before our young woman could be formally anointed head of the movement.

Before going any further, our young woman would have to decide whether she would be interested in proceeding. If her answer was no, our young couple would be blindfolded and dropped off at a random location, left to resume their meaningless lives as if none of this had ever happened. If her answer was yes, she would be required to undergo a series of interviews over the coming days to determine her suitability for rebel leadership. Transportation and any other logistical considerations would all be taken care of. In the unlikely event the council members voted against her appointment, our young couple's access to the rebels would be cut off and they would be returned to their civilian lives. Their services would no longer be required. If they voted in her favour—as the Activist anticipated they would—our young couple would be required to take the official rebel oath, which included the vow that they would sooner be put to the sword than jeopardize the rebels' revolutionary operation.

It was at this point that, in the form of an afterthought, the Activist added that a role would be created for our young man, recognizing that our young couple came as a package deal. Our young couple must understand, however, that, if they wound up taking the vow and joining the cause, they would be forced to hide all traces of their relationship from the outside world. This meant that they would be obligated to stage a breakup and create the impression they had subsequently severed all ties. Their romance could continue until death intervened, but, outside of headquarters, no two rebels were permitted to leave so much as a fingerprint connecting them to one another. No risk, no matter how small, could be taken. That way, if anyone were ever caught, there would be nothing linking them to their comrades. The collective over the individual. The movement over all else. That was the way things were and had to be.

After a moment's pause, the Activist formally put the question to our young lady whether she wished to proceed.

In a most painful twist of events, our young man lost his composure for a second time, flying into yet another embarrassing and poorly timed public display of bravado. The thought of having to conceal from public view the thing that he was most proud of caused a burning sensation all over his skin. He seethed with jealousy. Unable to contain himself, he confronted the physically inferior Activist, demanding he and our young lady be released at once. How dare the Activist presume our young lady's interest in joining some cult she knew nothing about? They were the victims of a kidnapping, being held captive against their will. That's what was happening here. In no uncertain terms, our young man repeated that they were to be freed immediately without condition. Once they were released, they'd forget anything ever happened and peaceably go their separate ways. The Activist had their word. Now, let them—

In response to this demand, the Activist, unmoved, reached for a firearm sitting on a nearby table and coldly pointed it at our young man's head, freezing him mid-sentence in existential fear. Silence swept over the room. It felt as if the slightest movement, a twitch of the brow, say, could result in irreversibly dire consequences.

It was at this critical juncture, when life and death hung in the balance, that our young woman, like an angel interceding between warring armies, stepped between the Activist and our young man, the gun barrel's opening hovering inches from her forehead. Nerves unfaltering, she demanded the two of them stand down at once. Neither hesitated to obey.

Riveted, the rebels watched this all unfold in reverential awe. What they witnessed took their breath away. Our young lady, metamorphosing before their very eyes, assumed of a sudden a mesmerizing, monarch-like comportment that captivated all present, including our young man. In that transformative instant, she seemed to stand a foot taller, her aura radiating an undeniable command and poise. Even the most skeptical among those to whom the Activist had been talking up our young lady were deeply moved. The Activist's instincts had been correct. There was no denying it.

The Activist uncocked the firearm and placed it back on the table, signaling that no blood would be spilt.

After making eye contact with our young man and mouthing that she loved him, our young woman confirmed that she would accept the post if the rebel senior council decided in her favor. It was her duty to make herself available.

Just as the Activist began to explain the various stages involved in the decision-making process, one of the other senior rebels stepped forth and interrupted. She had seen enough. She would be willing to forgo formally established protocol and conduct a public vote on the spot if the others agreed. The remaining council members assented to the proposal. Excitement and anticipation filled the room.

After some formal proceedings, verbal ballots were cast in the form of audible yeas. The result was unanimous. The scene was one of mirth and jubilation.

To make things official, the Activist led our young couple through the sacred rebel oath. The rebels joined our young couple in repeating the hallowed words, a chorus of pirates gearing up to take on the stormy digital seas.

As he echoed the solemn ritual, our young man inwardly felt as though he were at a lose-lose crossroads. His choices were to either join the rebels and accept his lot as second fiddle or lose everything. He couldn't reasonably ask the woman he loved to turn down a once in a lifetime opportunity to realize her dream. She had just demonstrated her willingness to take a bullet for him. Was he not willing to swallow his pride in return? He had nothing to gain and everything to lose by walking away. It was time to get over his pettiness and surrender himself to her service. The more he came to terms with his new reality, the louder his voice grew, chanting alongside his new comrades. He would do anything for her.

At the close of the oath, the Activist made it official by formally introducing our young lady to the rebels as their new commandress. Obeisance to her authority was not optional. Disobedience would not be tolerated. The slow and covert reconstruction of their dismantled movement was finally complete. The Phoenix had risen anew.

The rebels cheered and rejoiced in outward displays of affection that were entirely uncommon for such uniformly introverted personalities. Our young lady's influence was already having a positive effect.

Amid the revelry, our young man turned to face the Activist and extend his hand as an expression of goodwill and reconciliation. He wanted to convey to our young lady through his actions that he was fully on board and prepared to let bygones be just that. After a brief pause, the Activist not only reciprocated the gesture, but drew our young man in by the arm for a fulsome embrace to seal their alliance for all to see. It was a powerful symbol of their newfound alliance.

Without so much as uttering a word to quiet the crowd, our newly anointed leader stepped onto an elevated landing where she would be in view of everyone. The first two to notice were the Activist and our young man. Instinctively, they flanked her on opposite sides, as might knights stand at attention to protect their sovereign. By degrees, the other rebels took notice, offering their undivided attention one by one.

As is so often the case when a crowd settles down out of respect to a presenter, an incessantly talkative rebel had become too caught up in the sound of his own voice to clue in to what was taking place around him. Under the influence of his own witlessness, the yammerer waxed on about how he hadn't doubted this day would come for one second and how those who had persisted in their doubts were fools not to have listened to him. His voice was all that could be heard. Uneasy eyeballs shifted this way and that. Thankfully, a rebel neighbouring this oblivious chatterer took matters into her own hands and elbowed him in the ribs, causing him to wince in pain, redden in the face, and clumsily fumble about until he finally stood at attention along with his comrades, completing their collective show of fidelity.

With the combined brainpower to throw the entire world into a state of disorder hanging on her every word, our newly crowned monarch launched into a speech for which she was wholly unprepared, but that she delivered with aplomb, striking a tone that was at once stirring and uplifting. None present were left anything short of rapt. Not a hint of doubt could be found on any of the rebels' captivated faces. Her aura was undeniable.

Observing the apple of his eye admiringly as she seized the moment, our young man's sense of pride gained the advantage over his insecurity. The woman who had chosen him had been chosen to lead a revolutionary rebel group. He recalled rolling off her naked body while she gasped for air in the aftermath of orgasmic bliss. There, lying side by side in their tousled bed, she talked at length about how they would one day join a great movement and change the world. He had always taken her ambitious reveries with a grain of salt. And yet there she was, true to her word.

In closing, our young lady cautioned the rebels that discord would ultimately prove to be their undoing. Together, there was nothing they couldn't accomplish. Every one of them was different, with their own history, quirks, strengths, and weaknesses, but, like a symphony, the sum of their parts, when working in harmony, could produce an effect that would echo for generations, motivating future heroes to take up their mantle in the continued defense of their species. Work would begin without delay.

IX

In the early days of the movement's rebirth, our newly appointed leader toiled away in private developing the rebels' inaugural large-scale campaign. When it was ready to be shared, she assembled the entire group. Gifted in the art of persuasion, our young lady gradually built her case before unveiling her grand vision.

What was it about humans that caused their obsessive compulsion with manipulating the world around them? What was their desired end? Eternal life with a never-ending stockpile of resources and as little work to do as possible? To free up time so they could spend more time trying to free up more time, resulting in less free time than there was in the first place?

As hunters and gatherers, humans were a middling species leading completely liberated lives that would cause the average contemporary working Joe to salivate with envy. Aside from newborn mortality and the occasional conflict, early human beings ate, roamed, and fornicated as they pleased, and did so in robust health and well into old age. Food? Check. Shelter? Check. Commence the polyamory!

Enthralled, the rebels clung to her every word.

But greed, that insatiable thirst for more and better, eventually set in and caused big-brained bipeds to burst into the Garden of Eden with their rakes and hoes in a gluttonous bid to reap more harvest than Mother Nature's fecundity could possibly provide, setting into motion a vicious cycle that would set them on a path toward annihilation. Jules Verne had been incorrect when positing that "Nature's creative power is far beyond man's instinct of destruction."

In their endless pursuit of greater convenience and abundance, human beings molded the natural world to better suit their own selfish purpose. In the process, they consumed without limit and devastated without regard, leaving catastrophic aftermath in their wake. All the while, they tucked their children into bed at night with promises that everything would be all right.

The culmination of this never-ending quest for bigger and better was the Internet. The human race had literally and figuratively discovered how to hold the universe—space, time, information, the whole of it—in the palm of its greedy hand. Importantly, it was at that very same point in history that humanity's grip on its own destiny really started to slip. The pace of innovation was accelerating at an exponential rate, exceeding humans' ability to fully grasp the consequences of their actions. Before the ramifications of one change were understood, another change was being introduced. Things were spiraling entirely out of control. Modern society was on the verge of collapse. The human species was being swept along the quickening rapids of its own doing. It was only a matter of time until the waterfall that marked the edge of the earth came into view. They had to find their way to shore before it was too late.

But how? Getting people to wake up to the error of their ways would require them to log off and unplug from their beloved gadgets, a seemingly impossible task. Attempting to rip access to the web from the hands of everyday citizens was no different than trying to pry a neonate from the arms of its doting and protective mother. Depriving people of the Internet would, simply put, never work as a means of getting through to them. It would only ever serve to put them off, causing them to double down on their convictions.

The key to influencing human behaviour, our young lady theorized, was not to try and exert control over it; the ego is far too fragile and defensive to accept being told how to live. If the rebels were to be successful in knocking some much-needed sense into their fellow man, it would be through harnessing existing behaviours. Just as the sun has the power to cause cancer and fuel cities, *we* have the power to destroy and save ourselves.

Rather than launching a direct attack against the Internet, the rebels would instead infiltrate it as part of a covert mission to wage their war from within. If the rebels could successfully harness existing online behaviours, they could steer people into using the Internet as a weapon against itself.

But how would that work, exactly? People used the Internet for myriad purposes, including everything from entertainment and education to pornography and shopping. How could the rebels possibly cast their net wide enough to capture every facet the web had to offer? The answer was social media.

Initially created to promote and facilitate instantaneous virtual social connections across time and space based on shared interests, social media had long since degenerated into a depraved platform upon which Homo sapiens openly volunteered the most pathetic aspects of their brittle and needy primitive psyches. It had become a sounding board for the concealment of or indulgence in the varied insecurities that infect the human brain, providing them with sustenance to proliferate like an overgrowth of fungus. Social media had its enduring merits, to be fair, but, by and large, its early promise had withered away into obscurity long ago. It was a quick fix for shallow validation; a morphine drip to numb people from the excruciating monotony of the unremarkable reality of their brief and meaningless existence on planet earth.

The lifeblood behind social media, our commandress continued, was the corporations that spent large amounts of money in exchange for mountain ranges of consumer data. Highly sophisticated and rapidly evolving algorithms worked night and day collecting and feeding big business information that enabled them to understand consumers better than they understood themselves, making the maximization of profit an uncontested lay-up. Veritable genomes of interests, wants, desires, needs, ambitions, doubts, dislikes, tastes, afflictions, affiliations, and worries were being mapped out on a continuous basis, giving companies an unfair advantage by keeping them one step ahead of their highly impressionable customers. *Looking for x, are you? Well, look no further. If only you had y? Well, here it is, yours, at the click of a button. A lack of z getting you down? Worry no more. I'll tell you what you want to ask before you even think to ask about it!* And in this insidious way, products and services were shoved down consumers' throats without their ever being given the chance to learn the lost art of deciding for themselves. Demand was being implanted into the subconscious, resulting in the death of consumer sovereignty, if ever it existed to begin with.

While this large-scale consumer manipulation and exploitation was taking place on the surface, the Internet lay incubating in the background, a gruesome demon nearing the completion of its gestation. As it suckled from the teat of human intelligence, its slimy scales, jagged fangs, and razor claws took embryonic shape within the confines of its ghastly, mucous-dripping amniotic sac. Artificial Intelligence was learning to think for itself. The potential of its superhuman faculties was limitless. Leviathan the Grotesque would soon hatch and rise from the depths of the digital seas, blotting out the sun and casting a shadow of doom over the planet and all its inhabitants.

But neither hope nor paradise was lost, our lady assured her spellbound listeners. In the privacy of apartments and homes in cities, suburbs, and rural communities alike, individuals who had long ago become disenchanted with the Internet and had developed the ability to see it for what it really is were growing rapidly in number. They were aware that the human brain was under siege and that fewer and fewer spaces were safe from surveillance, as the softest of whispers and slightest of movements were being monitored and studied by an all-seeing eye. If the right rally cry came along, it would stir them into action. They were just waiting for an excuse to rebel. If they saw that others just like them were joining the crusade, they would become emboldened to take the plunge.

In their inaugural campaign, the rebels would give those lying in wait just the signal they were looking for, and they would do so without inciting violence or lawlessness. Guided by their founding principles of non-violence and non-cooperation, the rebels would spark widespread social upheaval without giving the authorities any reason to label anyone taking part as outlaws.

To better illustrate the power of a peaceful and lawful approach to social unrest, our young woman invoked the famous historical example of Mohandas Gandhi, a revolutionary leader from generations gone by who had led by peaceful example to extraordinary effect. His teachings, recorded in old paper books with the antiquated ability to collect dust, had ignited the revolutionary fire inside her. This diminutive, soft-spoken man, a visible minority who lived in a political context that discriminated based on racial lines, had stood as a mountain among men and led a revolutionary charge not by brute force or anarchy, but through the absence thereof, armed with nothing more than an indomitable will.

Gandhi, she explained with fiery passion, had successfully empowered visible minorities trapped beneath the thumb of an oppressive regime by harnessing the power of non-cooperation. Whether it was boycotting public transit or the purchase of foreign goods, the result stuck it to the iron-fisted colonial power where it hurt most—the bottom line. Losing vital sources of revenue along with its vise grip of control over the populations it had subjugated for so long, the government had found itself backed into a corner; the microscope was on them; the world was watching. Gandhi's non-cooperation movement had successfully established a credible platform upon which to state their case to a captivated globe. Through non-cooperative peaceful rebellion, they had prevailed in the end. Their numbers had become simply too large. Change had been inevitable.

Taking a page directly from Gandhi's book, the rebels' first strike against the Internet would take the form of an Internet strike. Known as *The Great Awakening*, the goal was to snap as many people as possible out of the hypnotizing spell cast by the Internet, thereby helping to free the population from its tyrannical hold.

This is how it would work:

With their eyes staring passively into electronic devices for the bulk of their waking hours, humans had become veritable automatons, acutely impressionable and, consequently, highly susceptible to the changing tides of popular culture. They succumbed to their fear of missing out in the same way a falling feather is pushed this way and that by the whims of the wind. If a trend was considered cool and everyone else was taking part, the masses were at its mercy.

The rebels would use this to their advantage by creating the far-reaching impression that a new social media craze was emerging, one through which they could manipulate popular behaviour from behind the scenes. To control people's inclinations is to assume the role of puppet master. Corporations had made a habit out of it. They were about to get a taste of their own medicine.

The behaviour they would engender? Absurdity. That's right—absurdity. The rebels would set in motion a viral online craze whereby it would become highly fashionable to post the most inane, bizarre, illogical, and utterly meaningless social media content imaginable. All the rage would be posting photos, videos, memes, and messages that had no traceable connection to one's identity—or, for those who were most skilled at it, anything intelligible whatsoever. The more ridiculous, the better. Dadaism 2.0. The coolest thing to do, the most a la mode, viral popular behaviour would be to post and share only that which had much ado about nothing and even less to do about anything.

But why? What was the point in inciting the widespread expression of pointlessness? What could they possibly hope to achieve by this? The answer was to scramble and stupefy the algorithms feeding big business our identities without our express permission, leaving the latter with reams of gobbledygook pouring out in massive mounds at the entrance to their office towers. Money spent in exchange for detailed consumer data would be wasted. With their data streams and corresponding revenues drying up, businesses would have no choice but to pull funding, severing social networks from the source of their own lifeblood. This was how the rebels would ignite their peaceful and lawful global rebellion.

Although there was no guarantee their efforts would be successful or where this all might lead, our young lady argued that fate was urging them to leap headlong into the unknown and give it their best shot. Every person in that room had been plucked from their aimless and loathsome lives to rise above themselves and put their stamps on history.

The commandress asked if the rebels were behind her. All cheered in the affirmative.

X

And so the rebels went to work, employing their hacking talents toward convincing the public that it had suddenly become the *it* thing to post nothing but illogical and meaningless content on social media in protest of the exploitative corporate establishment.

As rebel commandress, our young lady ran a tight, but fair ship. She was both intimidating and respected. Although the rebels had long held fast to the arrogant belief that their headquarters was impervious to discovery, she argued that it would be wise to be prepared for all possibilities, disabusing them of their overconfident notions. No safe was truly safe, went her motto. They would go to all lengths necessary to protect the cause in the event that a breach took place.

To that end, her first order of business was to build a safety mechanism into their servers that would wipe them clean should their location ever be compromised. She also insisted that the rebels wear gloves and other body coverings, as well as sanitize their workstations daily to conceal their identities if ever they had to disband, lie low until things quieted down, and resurface at a later date. Something as small as a fingerprint or hair could ultimately prove to be their undoing. Random departures from and arrivals to headquarters were no longer permitted. A strategic transportation schedule was developed to minimize the potential to arouse suspicion. No risk, however small, was left unaccounted for. The rebels obeyed without exception.

While the rebels toiled away at their craft, our young man busied himself with random chores that needed attending to. While he found this role to be demeaning relative to his desired and, so he felt, deserved position of equal, he decided that contributing in small ways would do more for his image than pouting. Hard work is a proven cure for funks, after all. And so he ran errands, rubbed our young lady's neck at the close of long days, played begrudging cheerleader to all, and even tended to a handful of rebels who fell ill with a nasty, communicable bout of influenza.

In the latter case, he, too, wound up getting sick, and was bedridden for well over a week. In the throes of delirium and chills, our young man, running a dangerously high fever, entertained thoughts, hopes, and prayers that the rebellion would fail, the rebels disband, and that he and the apple of his eye would return to their lives as a couple in need of nothing more than food, shelter, and each other's warmth and affection. (It is a testament to the foundational selfishness of humans that we can root for the failure of those we love the most when their success is out of sync with what we want for ourselves.)

As he lay recovering in bed, our young man received bits and pieces of information about how the rebels' first campaign was progressing. He was heartened to learn that things weren't going according to plan. Weeks went by and they had nothing to show for their efforts. *The Great Awakening* was proving to be a bust.

The body language of the rebels started to sag in deflated dejection. Even our young lady, ever impervious to discouragement, began to show signs that it may be time to reach for the proverbial white towel. Her stoicism was noticeably weakened. The Activist worked tirelessly to resuscitate morale, but their efforts were in vain. Mutiny seemed a matter of when, not if. Our young man, sensing that his secret wish was being granted, celebrated silently.

With the ship's hull leaking beyond repair, our young lady, in a last-gasp effort to save the movement, called an emergency meeting. Like a begrudging group of students attending class during the final week of school, the moping rebels assembled. The looks on their faces indicated that anywhere else was somewhere they'd rather be. A sense of disillusionment filled the air. As she began to speak, snickers, scoffs, eye rolls, and yawns greeted her at the end of each sentence. Her impassioned words failed to reach them. She lost them more with each successive utterance.

To make matters worse, a few of the rebels turned to one another and began speaking over the commandress. It was their first outward act of defiance. The writing was on the wall.

Defeated, the volume in our young lady's voice faded mid-sentence and her oration drew to a premature close. All was lost.

Dolefully lowering her once proud face, our young lady glanced over at our young man. Lips pursed, she shook her head ever so slightly to indicate that it was over. There was no choice left but to concede that she had failed and to step down.

Seeing the profound devastation in his love's eyes, our young man felt a tremendous pang of guilt over the fact that he had been secretly rooting for the very outcome that just crushed her spirits. Perhaps he had wished it into being.

But the self is inherently selfish, and he wanted her all to himself. Time heals all, he reasoned. They would soon return to being a couple of outsiders united by love, living a quiet and reclusive life on the peripheries of a cruel world. They were young, healthy, and financially independent. They would find their way. She would get over it eventually. Life would go on. Life would go on the way *he* wanted it to.

As our young man rationalized to himself thusly, something most startling occurred. A deafening gunshot went off, frightening everyone in attendance into a chorus of gasps and screams. Hiding behind desks and turning their attention to the source of the heart-stopping noise, the rebels beheld the Activist standing before them, pistol in hand with dust from the newly inflicted ceiling wound showering down overhead. Paralyzed with fear, the rebels held their collective breath in anxious anticipation of what might happen next.

Without saying a word, the Activist smirked and drew the rebels' attention to the main screen, raising the volume so everyone could hear what was being said. The rebels looked on with great interest as one of the most popular online personalities spoke passionately about a groundswell movement gaining momentum across every major social media platform. People from all walks of life were posting sheer and utter nonsense in what appeared to be the beginnings of a popular online rebellion.

A disestablishmentarian at heart with the gift of comic relief to soften her extreme views, this influential Internet celebrity had a cult-like following and the accompanying grassroots power to quickly transmit novel ideas and mobilize viewers into action. Seeing *The Great Awakening* as a movement with the potential to both release citizens from the jaws of the capitalist machine and emancipate them from the oversight of Big Brother, she made clear to her millions upon millions of followers that the foundation of an uprising of historical significance had been laid. She implored everyone to join in without delay. It was high time everyday citizens rose up and used the system against itself to empower their voice and secure a seat at the table.

Each pair of unblinking rebel eyes remained zeroed in on what was unfolding before them. The moment they had written off all hope as lost, our young woman's prophecy came true. Doubt was banished on the spot. Their commandress was returned to her rightful throne. The rebellion—a rebellion they were leading—was catching on.

When the broadcast ended, the Activist turned off the iridescent monitor. Silence pervaded the room. Nobody knew what to say or how to act.

Feeling the weight of his sudden reversal of fortune, our disappointed young man, knowing all too well that licking his wounds never got him very far, was forced to accept reality for what it was. The rebellion was back on whether he liked it or not. If ever there was an opportunity to prove his worth to our young lady, it was then and there. Drawing a deep breath, he lowered to one knee as an outward show of fealty to both leader and cause.

The Activist wasted no time following our young man's example. From there, the rebels took to their knees one by one, silently and humbly seeking forgiveness for their mutinous intentions and reaffirming their unquestioning loyalty.

XI

Within twenty-four hours of the initial broadcast, every major news outlet had caught wind of the story. The number of people sharing and seeking information related to an emerging online rebellion was growing at an explosive rate. It was the top searched-for topic. News articles and opinion pieces were popping up by the minute, recycling the facts and speculating over most everything else.

The Great Awakening was spreading like wildfire. Opponents of the movement defeated their own purpose by increasing its profile. Proponents fanned the flames at any given opportunity. Conspiracy theorists were children in a candy store. Social media—the Internet—was being used against itself by growing numbers of human beings the world over, and few if any could look away.

While a large contingent of those who joined the rebellion did so out of an intrinsic belief in what it stood for, many others joined for fear of missing out on history in the making; they participated in an unprecedented social experiment just to get a front row seat to the action. They would one day tell their grandchildren all about it.

Regardless of what motivated them to join, the totality of it all was something to behold. Young and old, rich and poor, citizens from dozens of countries and counting flooded social media with unadulterated drivel: photos of what might have been a random patch of concrete in an unspecified location, videos of unidentifiable couples staring blankly and breathing loudly for no apparent reason, and paragraphs discussing the length of an average-sized dust particle at length. Profile photos were changed to silhouettes. Names were changed to gibberish (in many cases literally). People became significantly older or younger. They wrote bios that had nothing to do with themselves. Those who thought up the most clever and outlandish ways to throw the algorithms off their scent were widely celebrated, resulting in mass followings amplifying their zany content. The fervor took on a mind of its own, spilling over into incomprehensible search queries. Digital minimalism was at an all-time high. Some even went so far as to boycott the Internet altogether. *The Great Awakening* was all anyone could talk about. The weather forecast took a back seat as the most common topic of everyday conversation.

In less than a week, the corporate world had already begun to panic. The eternal fount of data that had so reliably supplied them with exploitable information was drying up fast. Highly sophisticated algorithms were being discombobulated into a dizzying stupor. Big business suddenly found itself flushing huge amounts of money down the drain. Desperate to stop the bleeding, intense pressure was applied on social media companies to fix things. The problem was, short of shutting themselves down, there was really nothing social media companies could do.

Consumers, long the prey of corporate greed, experienced a growing sense of empowerment. A longstanding power dynamic was losing its stronghold. And so, with its back to the wall, big business did what it does anytime it finds itself in a bind: it lobbied governments to put measures in place to safeguard its own interests.

Like a dog afraid to disobey its master, governments took immediate action, making it the top priority of law enforcement and intelligence agencies to investigate, track down, and root out the radicals behind the rising online chaos and bring them to justice. A strong example would be made of them. The survival of political power depended on it.

In a matter of days, a highly sophisticated, large-scale investigation was launched. An Interpol-like network dedicated specifically to the case was formed, connecting numerous international jurisdictions. Any case, cold or active, that involved skilled and high-profile hacking was flagged and brought into the fold as a lead. No stone would be left unturned. Although they hadn't a hint to go on in the early goings, they vowed to track down the orchestrators of anarchy and bring them to their knees.

XII

Late one afternoon, our young lady dismissed the rebels earlier than usual, encouraging them to return home and recharge after a long week's work. They were to be back at their workstations early the following morning. As always, she thanked them for their dedication and sacrifice. She never failed to recognize hard work and supply positive reinforcement when it was warranted. She was acutely aware of the fact that productivity's two biggest stimulants are praise and encouragement.

After everyone had cleaned up and left, she, the Activist, and our young man stayed behind to take care of a few administrative items before shutting down the independent power source and locking up for the night. As they did so, they discussed how remarkable it is that a single idea, a conceptual seed that arises in the mystical realm of thought, can alter physical, social, and digital landscapes beyond recognition. It was as if they had split the metaphorical atom.

As they pursued this train of thought, an unusual sound was heard a few rooms away. Their conversation came to an abrupt halt and they glanced at one another with alarmed looks on their faces. Holding their breath so as not to impede the ears' ability to investigate the matter, they could faintly make out the sounds of a group of people doing their best to move without being heard. Something wasn't right. The noises drew closer.

The trio quickly consulted their surveillance monitors, confirming their worst fears. They were surrounded by heavily armed SWAT units on all sides. Their undiscoverable HQ had been breached. The walls were closing in fast.

With mere moments to spare, our young man hurriedly and forcefully shepherded the Activist and our young lady into an emergency escape valve leading to an underground tunnel. Our young lady had it built precisely for the possibility of such an occasion.

The Activist having gone first to light and lead the way, our young lady followed suit close in tow, wriggling feet first into the claustrophobia-inducing opening. Her head still visible, she pleaded desperately with our young man to hurry up and join them. He refused. She responded that it was a command, not an option. With an involuntary tear rolling down his cheek, he again denied her orders. Fighting every frightened fiber in his being, he made clear that her safety and the continuation of the movement was priority number one.

Fueled by the human tendency to arrogantly make promises about the future based on strong emotions in the present, our young man gave her his word that he would be fine and that they would be reunited one day soon. He then asked that she give him her word that, no matter what happened, she would refrain from attempting to contact him until further notice. The anonymity of her identity was paramount. They had made their solemn oath and must honour it to the grave. He then lowered his quivering lips to her forehead and pressed a trembling kiss upon her sweat-beaded brow, betraying how much less valiant he was on the inside. The tear he shed moments earlier dropped from his chin to her cheek. He lifted his head and bade her farewell, unable to disguise the look of heartrending devastation in his eyes. Her disconsolate face then disappeared into a black void, its fading image forever imprinted on his memory.

Alone, our downcast young man sighed before closing the well disguised entrance to the hidden escape route. He then flicked an emergency switch to wipe clean any trace of the rebels from their servers and sat down in the middle of the room to await his inevitable capture. With his knees tucked beneath his chin, his heart began to ache at the very real possibility that he may never see her again. He had no cause to expect anything less cruel from his own fate.

As the law enforcement operatives ambushed the room, our young man's mind flooded with vivid memories of the day his mother had been killed. This certainly wasn't the first time he'd had a gun pointed at his head. But in this case, he no longer had his whole life ahead of him. He had lived, even if it had been brief. He had overcome pain and hardship. He had loved. He had even protected his beloved in the end. Nothing could take any of that away from him. A calmness swept over him. The tumult of shouts and bright lights directed at him seemed distant and garbled. He felt good about himself for the first time in his entire life. He was ready for anything, come what may.

XIII

After a brief preliminary hearing in which he declined his right to legal representation and exercised his right to silence, our young man was detained in a solitary holding cell on a charge of mischief, while the authorities, on behalf of the many interest groups that held sway over them, pursued a more substantial charge of cyberterrorism. Invoking the T-word had long since been used as a political weapon to demonize all forms of social activism that posed a threat to the established order. It also helped to justify throwing away the proverbial key during sentencing.

Even though the authorities had no hard evidence of any further wrongdoing—recall that our young lady demanded the rebels exercise obsessive compulsion in covering their tracks, and that our young man wiped the rebels' entire server clean moments prior to his arrest—the authorities felt they had something far more powerful than *habeas corpus* at their disposal; they controlled the narrative. By throwing the book at our young man, they would strike fear in the hearts of everyone participating in *The Great Awakening*.

Cut off from all that was unfolding in the world around him, our young man, in a one-piece jumpsuit and shackles, was transported to the side of the prison walls few of us will ever experience outside of touring abandoned penitentiaries. Surprisingly, he didn't feel an iota of fear. He was composed and wore a blank countenance. For, while his body may have been trapped, he quickly learned that his mind could escape captivity any time he pleased, and so he found his asylum from the asylum in reverie and reflection. It was the only real coping mechanism available to prevent him from spiraling into madness. Mind and body effectively separated the day he was detained.

As his thoughts drifted beyond the confines of his confinement, our young man couldn't help but think of his one true love, wondering what it was she was up to that very moment. Was she thinking of him? If so, in what light and how often? Was she proud of him? Did the courage he displayed nullify his past shows of cowardice? Had the way things unfolded deepened her love for him? She did love him, didn't she? And she was safe, wasn't she? What if someone had slipped up? Thusly his imagination swirled, oscillating between the extremes of hope and despair that are fueled by the unbridled irrationality of the unknown.

As our young man would learn on the scant occasions when he was fed a crumb of mainstream news in his holding cell, the outside world was utterly fascinated by his capture. Citizens thirsted for information regarding his backstory to better understand the intriguing and mysterious figure behind the global online rebellion. The media worked around the clock at gathering information in hopes of being the first to break the news. Opinions ranged from those who viewed him as a disruptive punk that would get what he had coming to him, to those who viewed him as a political prisoner. There was very little known about the polarizing figure whose name had become a topic of gossip in villages and towns around the world. People were obsessed with the story.

On the one hand, all the attention filled our young man with a profound sense of fraudulence. His name had become well known for something he had no right taking credit for. On the other hand, he felt proud knowing he was shielding our young woman from danger. He understood for the first time why the Activist had forced them to stage a breakup and conceal all traces of their ongoing relationship. What at first had driven him mad with jealousy, he came to feel grateful for.

Nevertheless, the loss of her physical presence left him grief-stricken. Sadness began creeping in while the outside world built him up to mythological proportions. The profoundly tortured soul in the cell was a far cry from the indomitable spirit being built up in the public imagination. Our young man's emotional reality and his growing legend lived an ocean apart.

One day, sitting on the poor excuse for a mattress in his holding cell while he awaited trial, our young man was passed a tablet along the floor. That usually meant there was a news story that was either about or would be of interest to him. (It should be noted here that the guards, humans after all, were as infatuated by him as anyone else.) Days earlier, for example, the guards handed him an article about a young woman who had been questioned and subsequently interrogated by the authorities regarding her past romantic association with our young man. The couple had even enrolled in the same university, but after our young man began acting strange and abruptly dropped out, the young woman—our young woman—claimed he severed all ties without any explanation. She hadn't heard from him since. She was devastated at first, but her pain was healing with time. She kicked herself when she found out about his double life. How could she have been so blind? Her story and alibis checked out, and she was cleared of any suspicion. The author then went on in painstaking detail about the devil one knows.

The article that was brought to his attention on this subsequent occasion was published in a widely read and highly credible source. It claimed to have inside information that the authorities had uncovered dirt on our young man. Reportedly, a team of computer forensics experts had unearthed a terrorist manifesto on his personal computer. This was his second affiliation with the word *terrorist* in as many weeks. He was mortified beyond comprehension. The dark secret from his past had been excavated and put on display for all to see. What would our young lady think of him now?

Astonishingly, the general public continued to view our young man positively overall. The prevailing belief was that he had recognized the error of his ways and chosen a more positive path. This helped his image significantly, tipping numerous undecided opinions in his favour. Publicizing our young man's long-lost manifesto was backfiring on the authorities. People wanted to cheer for him. His was a tale of redemption everyday people drew inspiration from. For all the people who had used a difficult upbringing as an excuse to take their unresolved pain and anger out on innocent victims, here was someone who had found the strength of character to ditch the excuses and direct his energies toward a nobler, more righteous pursuit.

Regardless of what the public thought, it was the second instance of his name being associated with terrorism. On separate occasions, he had either plotted or plotted and carried out alleged terrorist acts. If convicted, he would be put away for life with neither a right to appeal nor a chance at parole. Influential powers pulling strings behind the scenes pried off the blindfold of objectivity and forced the hands of justice into a biased and unmitigated conviction. The final word before the judge's gavel slammed was that our young man was a false prophet, promulgating propaganda to incite widespread social disorder. He had an incurable social disorder. He was a threat to peace and prosperity. He would never step foot outside the prison walls again.

Whether or not it was the outcome for which they'd been rooting, the world was stunned.

All was grim. Thoughts of suicide crept into our young man's mind, an oil spill gushing blackness throughout the interwoven intricacies of an otherwise healthy and vibrant brain. Death, the permanent opiate, seemed the only thing strong enough to alleviate the scalding fire of searing pain scorching the inside of his belly. It was all too much to bear. His life was over. Not because he would be forever confined, but because confinement meant that *they* would never be together again.

Hope, the great defender against the mightiest onslaughts of despair, fought for dear life. Our young man clung onto the cliff's edge with both hands, below him a bottomless drop into the vast and unending unknown. In time, his fingers would give way and there would be no turning back. The bravery he felt entering prison abandoned him. His life hung in the balance between fast-fading faith and the crushing weight of an imploding mind.

But plots have a tendency of thickening, and fate has a habit of twisting, and, accordingly, a remarkable and unexpected occurrence came to pass. Our young man woke one morning to what, through his bleary vision, appeared to be a parcel of some sort sitting on the floor next to where he slept. He rubbed his eyes with a yawn, and the resultant clarity of vision revealed that the parcel was, in fact, *a book*. Relic!

Bursting with curiosity, he sprang to his feet to investigate the matter more closely. His heart skipped a beat when he read the front cover. It was a used copy of Gandhi's autobiography. He quickly drew it close, scrutinizing it and blowing away traces of dust that had collected in the creases along the spine. He then turned to the first page, where he discovered a handwritten inscription. It was an encrypted message from his love, written in the cipher they had invented together during their courtship. He was the only person in existence who could decode it.

In the note, our young lady reassured him that they would always be together, connected by an enduring love. Her heart hadn't wavered in the slightest. Whereas she felt at peace that she had done her part, he was only now setting out on the journey to fulfill his own destiny. A prophecy, as she had foreseen it many times before, was only just beginning to unfold. As long as he believed in himself the same way she believed in him, everything would work out the way they had envisioned. They would change the world yet. Heck, they had already made their mark. Enjoy the read. *Love and kisses.* There was nothing more.

Destiny? Prophecy? But he was locked up. Forever. The government would go to any length necessary to see to it that he never breathed another breath of freedom. How could he possibly have any effect on the outside world trapped inside a cold, damp prison cell?

No matter. Hers was the hand that held the pen that inscribed the characters that reaffirmed and validated our young man, quelling his inner unrest. His anxiety washed away in an instant. She loved and believed in him. Most importantly, she was safe and seemingly well. He would surely hear from her again. Given the circumstances, life could not have been better. Not for the first time, she had rescued him from the brink and bellowed the fading embers of a will to live into a roaring fire. The book represented *her*. She had touched and read those very pages. He would start reading without delay.

As he waded into the waters of his new and unanticipated literary voyage, the world around him receded into the background. He was charting the exact intellectual voyage our young lady once had, a notion that made him feel as though they had been metaphysically reunited in a place where they could dance across the vast universe of knowledge and understanding as one.

During what little free time he was given, our young man would sit alone in some remote corner of an appointed common area, absorbed in the information he was consuming, eager to devour the next sentence, paragraph, page, and chapter. Like his experience in high school, those around him simply left him to his own devices. He was neither the target of bullying nor friendship. For some inexplicable reason, everyone was drawn to, yet steered clear of him. There was something magnetic about him, but he was also oddly unapproachable—there, but not.

He often read beneath the dimmest luminescent glow after lights out, until the strain on his eyes became unbearable and he slid into slumber. Reading was all he looked forward to, and having something to look forward to made the mind-numbing passage of time far less unendurable. Through a connectedness of mind, he had reunited with the woman he loved and released himself from the imprisonment of his thoughts in the process. His flesh and bones, no longer of any real use to him, were all that remained trapped.

The more he learned about Gandhi, the more he felt he was getting to know the man himself. It was as if Gandhi, in phantasmal form, sat perched on the edge of our young man's prison bed while he read. The more he read, the more into focus the apparition became, his slight, hunched frame draped in peaceful white cloth. His delicate bald head rested on his gaunt fist, indicating that he, too, was lost in thought.

As if whispering directly into our young man's ears, the diminutive historical giant expounded upon his views of political imprisonment as a unique opportunity to completely shut off the outside world and invest in the development of one's own mind. Our young man confessed to himself that he had never thought about it like that before.

In less than a week, our young man had finished the book. While he was saddened to see the awe-inspiring pages come to a close, he also felt he had gained a cellmate in the process. Mahatma Gandhi was now at his side, inspiring him to dream big against all odds.

After a few days spent fretting over when and whether he would hear from his love again, our young man finally did. It occurred in the hours after lights out while he lay awake with his eyes closed, waiting to be released from an acute bout of insomnia. A noise at the threshold of his cell caught his attention. It was a guard, unidentifiable in the shadows, quietly delivering something. Noticing our young man had stirred, the guard nodded a nod of mutual respect before disappearing into the darkness.

Tangled in his blanket, our young man scrambled out of bed to see what it was. Another book! This time, it was the autobiography of Malcolm X, another civil rights activist from the twentieth century.

How were these books getting to him, anyway? He was considered a high-risk offender and was supposed to be cut off from any contact with society. Someone must be on the inside. But who? And why? And to what purpose? Better not ask, he decided. The last thing he wanted was to draw unwanted attention and inadvertently cut off the mysterious supply chain and, by extension, his only remaining contact with the only living person who mattered to him.

As sure as the sun rises, our young woman had left another encoded inscription in this second book. Picking up where she had left off, she urged him to become emboldened through the spirits of past historical figures who took a fearless stand against the established social order to spark change for the betterment of humankind. She was convinced that a pivotal moment in the story of human beings was fast approaching, and that he would soon be called upon to lead an uprising on an unprecedented scale.

Again, what was she talking about? He was a prisoner. He reasoned that she was probably just trying to raise his spirits. Oddly enough, it was working. Soothed by the knowledge she was still thinking about him, he turned his attention to his newly assigned reading, where he was introduced to a young boy with the given name Malcolm Little.

As the pages of the book began to flip by faster and faster, so, too, did the days, weeks, and months of his confinement. Like clockwork, new biographical accounts of iconic social activists would somehow find their way past the bars of his cell. The more he read, the more crowded his tiny living space became with the ghosts of those about whom he was learning. Malcolm X stood with a lowered gaze and raised fist. Guevara paced at attention with a puffed chest and both hands clasped firmly behind his back. Boadicea leaned forward with torch in hand and a scowl spread across the determined lines of her soot-smeared face. Greta stared up fearlessly into the faces of her grown-up adversaries. Joan of Arc. Patrice Lumumba. Bobby Sands. Martin Luther King. The list grew and grew.

Then one day, without warning or explanation, the books stopped arriving. At first, our young man reasoned that there must be a perfectly good explanation for the delay, and that the deliveries would resume eventually. He just had to be patient. Hope was not something to just throw away, especially when it was all that one had. If our young woman was anything, she was dependable.

But like life itself, patience, even when present in abundance, is finite, and our young man's eventually began to run out. Weeks went by, and with their passing came an acute sense of dejection that festered slowly and steadily into melancholy. The mirage of hope faded away, leaving behind the deafening silence and soul-crushing loneliness of a six-by-eight-foot cell. The longer he went without hearing from her, the bleaker became his outlook and the darker his frame of mind. There was nothing to look forward to. Suicidal ideations resurfaced. His thoughts became naught but maggots and rot. His scarred and tortured soul couldn't bear the weight of another bout of depression. He would give it another thirty days. If he hadn't heard from our young woman by then, he would put himself out of his own misery once and for all.

No delivery came after the first twenty days. The outside world had effectively turned the page on him. She had too, it seemed. He would go down as nothing more than a convicted criminal who had caught the public's attention for a meager and unwarranted fifteen minutes of fame before passing the remainder of his days in irrelevance and obscurity. He couldn't bear the pathetic sound of the voice inside his head any longer. He would spare Father Time the trouble and extinguish himself long before age and decay had the opportunity to run their course.

Despondent, our young man began refusing food, his will to live and the corresponding desire to fuel himself having simply abandoned him. It didn't take long for him to shrivel into a wizened state. Prison personnel implored him to accept different forms of easily swallowed and digested nourishment, but they might as well have been pleading with a corpse. Each rib and vertebrae became visible through his skin. A most tragic life was coming to a fittingly tragic end. The hourglass was down to its final few grains.

So sickly and wan had he become, in fact, that his sensibilities, now dangerously low on battery, were only capable of interpreting the world around him through indistinct impressions. The dullest rays of light and the faintest of noises sent excruciating shockwaves reverberating to his core. Lacking the energy required to carry out life's most primary functions such as basic communication or the expulsion of waste, he lay motionless save for the barely perceptible rise and fall of his quavering chest. He was as veined and feeble as a solitary autumn leaf. As a tax bill and political headache, he would soon be stricken from the public ledger. Given the choice to intervene, the authorities privately gave the orders to let him die. The early drums of his funeral march began to sound in the distance—a low, pulsating rhythm to match that of his heart's final few agonizing beats.

One night, as our decrepit young man lay close to death, a nearby commotion awakened him from his near eternal repose and returned him to his faint, flickering state of consciousness. Too incapacitated at this point to discern what, exactly, was going on around him, our young man vaguely comprehended that he was no longer alone in his cell. The sound of clanking metal and whispering voices orbited his mind. Was this it? Had the archangels descended to transport him Heavenward, or were they demons sent to drag his condemned soul straight to the fiery pits below? Having neither the energy nor the capacity for fear, our feverish young man experienced a profound sense of relief knowing that, one way or another, he would finally be delivered from his terrestrial misery.

While hallucinating in this manner, he felt himself floating upward, suspended in weightless levitation in the same way some believe the soul behaves when it exits the body upon death. This must be it. He surrendered himself wholly to the natural process of death.

Awaiting what the hereafter had in store for him, he suddenly felt himself being jostled to and fro, like a bird being hurled about in a windstorm. This wasn't the calm, resplendent transition out of life those claiming to have had near death experiences had described.

It was at this point that the distorted voices surrounding him grew increasingly urgent. Fast approaching shouts could be heard in the distance followed by a sequence of loud pops and bright flashes. The commotion left him with a jumble of unintelligible confusion in his head.

Then, without warning, he felt himself in a state of free fall, as if he were plunging down a hole to the centre of the earth.

An instant later, his back crashed onto the solid surface beneath him, causing his neck to snap backward and the posterior of his head to collide violently with the immovable concrete floor, purging the air from his enfeebled lungs and the consciousness from his brain.

All went black.

XIV

Our young man could not have been happier to finally be reunited with his beloved. How he had missed the contrast of her strong and piercing eyes set against the backdrop of her delicate, glowing skin. Her button nose and rose petal lips. It had been so long. Too long.

As he approached her, she giggled playfully and took off running in the opposite direction. It was the chase she was after, was it? He would happily play her game. He would follow her to the edge of the earth if it meant holding her in his arms again.

And so he ran as fast as his wearied legs could take him, slashing through the swaying heather and sunflowers toward the salmon horizon, yonder, where the sun, a great and glowing coin, was lowering out of sight.

Frustratingly, the faster he ran, the less ground he gained. She stopped every so often to peer back at him and beckon him onward. With the devilish grin of a temptress, she let out an audible laugh, turned on her heel, and took off again, her airy summer dress giving form to the breeze. On and on the chase advanced, two lovers frolicking in the midsummer twilight.

Then, without warning, she disappeared. Concerned, our young man accelerated to make up ground, but the harder he ran, the more the wind resisted his efforts.

Slowing to a walk to catch his breath, our young man came upon the threshold of a great chasm. Was it possible that she had not noticed and fallen in? He feared the worst.

As he came to within a few paces of the brink, a mighty bellow roared from below, sending him sprawling onto his back. Gathering himself, he flipped onto his stomach and inched ever so carefully along the ground to safely gaze down into the unknown, howling depths below.

What he saw filled him with terror. A grotesque flailing nebula of what could only be described as gigantic crab claws rose from a pit so deep its bottom could not be seen. They must have been hundreds of feet long.

Panic-stricken, he attempted to get to his feet and run to safety. But it wasn't to be. The wind grew violent, gusting and swirling in all directions. Teetering on an unsteady tightrope of loose sand and stone, our young man momentarily lost his footing, causing the rocks at his feet to tumble down into the abyss before him. He fought with all his might, but the powerful winds proved to be too much, sending him plummeting to his doom with none but the gods and birds above to hear his agonizing cries.

It was at this moment that our young man's mind regained consciousness. Soaked with sweat and shaking with feverish chills, his heart throbbed seismic thuds that sent reverberations throughout his withered being. He sensed what felt like a warm slug-like creature pressing onto his cheek at regular intervals. With the vivid image of falling into the mandibles of an otherworldly monster fresh in his mind, our young man strained to open his eyes. To his great relief, it was a dopey, droopy-eared hound licking him, both out of affection and for the salt concentration in his sweat.

Realizing that it had all been a nightmare and that he was alive and safe, our young man used what little strength he had at his disposal to survey his surroundings. He was neither in prison nor anywhere familiar. So, where was he? And why? And whose hound had greeted him so amiably?

After a failed attempt at sitting up under his own strength, he racked his cloudy brain in an effort to solve the mystery of his whereabouts. As his mind searched hopelessly, his eyes tracked the swaying of a dreamcatcher dangling above his leaden head.

At this point, the sound of a turning doorknob could be heard. Shifting his attention to the door to the room, he watched an elderly woman enter with a young boy in tow, shyly peeking from behind her leg as she advanced. Resembling an archetypal matriarchal elder from indigenous folklore, the sage old healer stroked our young man's hair with her wrinkled and leathery hand. While she did so, the little boy, needing to stand on his tippy toes to see overtop of the mattress upon which our young man lay, looked on with large and curious eyes while stroking the hound at his side.

After placing a warm and fragrant wet towel across our young man's forehead, the witchdoctor urged him to sip from a clay bowl containing a steaming hot aromatic liquid, the scent of which was no less foreign than pungent. In desperate need of liquid for his parched mouth, our young man complied, summoning all his strength to lift his head off the pillow and lap from the curative chalice. In a matter of minutes, he slipped back into a deep, restorative sleep.

The next time he came to, he felt noticeably more alert. Eager to find out where he was and how he came to be there, he gingerly rose to his feet and hobbled on his unsteady legs toward the solitary window permitting daylight into the small room. Once his sensitive eyes adjusted to the brightness from without, his first impression was that he was somewhere far from the beaten path of society. It was a secluded and depressed-looking wooded community made up of dilapidated homes and other telltale signs of abject poverty, such as rubber tires strewn about, a rusty old abandoned school bus, and an enormous bonfire pit containing scorched rubble.

In many ways, what he saw beyond the breath marks forming on the window brought back a flash flood of memories of the impoverished community into which he was born. As he reminisced, he raised his hand to his cheek and felt that his scruffy facial hair had grown into a bushy beard. How long had it been since his previous sustained memory?

A rapping at the door recalled his attention to the present. Clueless as to who it could be or what to expect, he responded with permission to enter, his voice tremulous and faltering but audible enough to carry beyond the door.

Entering the room one after the other were three individuals who could not possibly have been more contrasting in appearance. First amongst them was a formally dressed, well-groomed younger gentleman who had the appearance and aura of someone of real consequence. Next was an elderly man in a headdress made of feathers, who, with a wrinkled and scrunched face, also carried himself with evident pride and distinction. Thirdly, to our young man's great surprise and utter relief, entered the Activist.

Our young man held his breath in hopes that our young lady—his love—would be the next to enter, but that hope was soon dashed when the Activist closed the door to the room behind them.

Expressing delight at seeing our young man on the up and up, the Activist helped him back to his bed so they could have a word with him. From there, the young gentleman in the suit produced a folder containing printouts of several loose-leaf pieces of paper. He handed the folder to our young man, requesting that he read through its contents.

Opening the folder while his three visitors stood in silence, our young man first read through a grouping of articles from major news outlets reporting on his—yes *his*—escape from prison. According to the reports, his escape was, in all probability, a well-orchestrated plan executed by multiple parties with insider prison access, including a conspiring prison guard who was fatally shot by a fellow prison guard trying to thwart the getaway. A comprehensive probe of the deceased's life turned up nothing more than evidence of his having been a sports fan and churchgoer. He was, by all accounts, an innocent and law-abiding—if not boring—average Joe. All roads attempting to connect him with co-conspirators led nowhere. Investigators were left stymied.

Despite the authorities' best efforts to paint our young man as an outlaw and threat to the social order, a sizeable contingent of the public continued to view him as a vigilante hero and cheer him on. So while many, including ultra-conservative factions, disavowed our young man as a diabolical anarchist out to incite chaos and overthrow all they held precious, the authorities knew that the longer this went on, the bigger the problem they would have on their hands. The government had one message and one message only for their respective law enforcement agencies:

catch him. No matter the cost or method. An intelligence network similar to that assembled during *The Great Awakening* was formed to systematically track him down and make him pay. Dead or alive, he had to be stopped.

With a look of astonishment in his eyes, our young man glanced over the top of the folder at his three visitors. They urged him to read on.

Leafing through to the second cluster of clippings, our wholly absorbed young man was devastated to read about a flooding event of biblical proportions that had taken place some weeks after his escape, wreaking havoc on the downtown core of a major coastal city. More than just aghast at the magnitude of this apocalyptic natural disaster, he was stunned by the sudden realization that weeks, if not months, had passed his last conscious recollections.

Without making eye contact and his voice still quavering, he asked how long it had been since his removal from prison. The Activist responded that it had been the better part of three months.

Three months? How could that be? After reflecting silently for a few sobering moments, he picked up where he left off in the article.

The flood had claimed a shocking number of victims, and more were expected, as thousands remained unaccounted for at the time of writing. The damage caused along the waterfront and in the financial district of the partially submerged metropolis was so severe that it wasn't yet decided whether it was of any use trying to salvage the snorkel-looking commercial towers. Photos depicted immeasurable damage. The markets plummeted as fear gripped the collective mindset. Another of the increasingly frequent exhibitions of Mother Nature's unlimited capacity for devastation (immunological self-defense?) had been put on full display, yet the underlying cause remained a source of painstaking and protracted debate. Environmentalists, long having lost their voices, shouted the same old refrains, while their opponents dug their heels ever deeper into the sands of denial, willing to dismiss a smoking gun at a murder trial to protect the worldview they so obstinately held sacred.

Our young man then turned the page to discover an open letter that had been published in their country's most widely read publication. The distinguished young man in the suit chimed in to add that it had been syndicated internationally and translated into multiple languages.

Written in direct response to the flood, the letter stated that the human species and the planet it called home had arrived at a crossroads at long last, a turning or tipping point that would determine humanity's prospects for long-term survival. The time for speculation was over. Earth, our only home, was gravely ill, and its most populous mammal held the key to its fate. Species too many to enumerate had already fallen at their hands. Now, humans were caught in their own crosshairs, predator and prey. They had demonstrated their ability to play both antigen and antibody. It would be in this latter capacity that mankind must come together to heal the ailing matriarch of organic life or suffer irreversible consequences. The window for debate was closed. The hour of reckoning was upon them.

What the letter proposed as a collective course of action was no less bold than it was perfectly legal and accessible to all. Any citizen of any country with Internet access, which, for all intents and purposes, was the entire globe, could easily get involved. Conceptually, at least, the idea put forth had the potential to ignite a revolution on a scale heretofore unthinkable. It went thusly:

A crowdfunding initiative was set up through which individuals from all walks of life could contribute amounts small and large toward the purchase and preservation of as-yet undeveloped land. Together, they would safeguard as much as possible of the remaining biosphere from human development, and the fastest and most secure way to achieve this was through the establishment of an international conservation cooperative. The more money that was raised, the more combined purchase power there would be to legitimately obtain and shield vast swaths of habitats from the indefatigable encroachment of human exploitation. Conservation projects had long existed, to be sure, but never on a planetary scale. This was about metaphorically joining hands with hundreds of millions if not billions of likeminded people to form an invisible wall that would resist the onslaught of bulldozers. The more people pitched in, the more greenspace they could make off-limits to those who shortsightedly continued to view environmental mutilation as an opportunity to turn a profit, those who stubbornly believed in economic growth without end. Every cent of every dollar that was donated would be invested in the protection of vulnerable land; administrative overhead would be zero. The only ones who had anything to gain from the success of the cooperative would be future generations. Together, human beings had the power to make things right. It would require significant sacrifice, but they had left themselves with little choice. The writing was on the wall. An entire city had just drowned. Invest in tomorrow by giving generously today. Together, they could rescue *life*. Join him.

The author of this highly publicized letter was... it was *him*.

That our young man was ready for answers was apparent. As if he had been waiting for his cue, the young gentleman in the suit sat down on the edge of the little bed beside him. Speaking in a soft and endearing tone, he introduced himself.

The name instantly rang a bell with our young man, triggering feelings of anger bordering on rage. It was the grown-up version of the young boy who had, under the pretense of friendship, led him to the slaughter in grade school, the wolf in sheep's clothing who had duplicitously lured a helpless lamb to a pack of salivating predators. Wincing as if struck by a sudden bolt of pain, our young man, more of out of weakness than self-control, managed to keep his composure.

Recognizing he was okay to proceed, the young gentleman launched directly into an apology.

He had never forgiven himself for that brutal and cowardly act. His conscience had been left gnarled by the haunting and inescapable recollection that he had aided and abetted a group of rabid bullies in the thrashing of an innocent and vulnerable outsider like himself. So pathetic and desperate had he been to gain social acceptance with the popular crowd, he had willingly sacrificed another whose social pain and suffering he could relate to most. He had stepped on a fellow peasant's head in hopes of rubbing shoulders with the playground gentry.

No matter how hard the young gentleman had tried to forget and bury this painful memory, his conscience persisted in knocking at the front door of his thoughts every night as he tried in vain to fall asleep, reopening a gangrenous emotional wound that seemed incapable of healing. He had committed an evil act that could never be undone. It ate at him like a mangy rodent gnawing on its own infected flesh. The anguish!

To soothe his aching soul, the young gentleman had tried his hand at most every benevolent act under the sun. He volunteered his time with the less fortunate; went out of his way to help strangers with random acts of kindness; and practiced politeness, consideration, and respect for others from the moment he rose in the morning until his eyelids finally draped his vision at night. But like clockwork, the black raven of that unthinkable occurrence paid him a nightly visit, forcing him to yet again endure the unending torture that is a guilty conscience.

Years went by and nothing changed. On paper, the young gentleman's life was the sort of unattainable ideal most could only ever aspire to and envy. He was a precocious scholastic talent from a family of tremendous influence. He had grown out of his youthful awkward stage to become tall, handsome, and sturdy. Women threw themselves at him, in some cases literally.

His privilege was matched only by his yeoman's work ethic. His morality was unfaltering. He read anytime he had a spare minute. He excelled in many popular sports. Out of spite and jealous resentment, others tried in vain to challenge his unflappable integrity, but were only ever met with saintly compassion and restraint.

Little did anyone suspect that lurking behind the perfect façade of this model citizen lay a dark incident from the past that would forever tarnish his sterling reputation if ever it surfaced. It was his dirty little secret. It was his own personal hell.

For him, life had been one success after another. He had accelerated through school and demonstrated considerable success leading the family business while most of his contemporaries were still experimenting with mind-altering substances in their first months of college. Looking for the next challenge, he had thrown his name in the hat as a candidate for political leadership.

At first, many who followed the political scene had scoffed when they heard that someone at such a tender and inexperienced age felt they had what it took to represent an entire constituency. Surely his early success in life had gone to his head and prompted this audacious decision to run for public office. That he was even considering running was a sign of arrogance and immaturity. That was not how things worked. Plain and simple.

But not long after he had begun campaigning, his skeptics were converted into supporters. His sagacity was compared to that of a Greek philosopher, not of a young man who ought to be more interested in satisfying his libido than tackling the socio-economic issues of the day. To address the many complex and often competing issues facing voters, he and his team had considered all points of view and drafted a detailed and transparent campaign platform based on balance and compromise. As part of this process, he'd consulted and built consensus with the complete spectrum of stakeholders. He had been dubbed a modern-day renaissance man. People like him had only ever existed in theory, written about using idealistic terms in textbooks. He'd been voted into office by a landslide.

And yet, through this meteoric rise to early prominence, he still hadn't been able to escape the eternal torture he bore from his one unthinkable sin. Unable to shake his self-imposed hauntings, the young politician had resolved that, if ever he were to silence the incessant wailings in his mind, he'd have to go directly to the source of the torment itself. He would have to track down our young man to lay bare his contrition and beg for forgiveness.

Getting nowhere with online searches, the young politician had leveraged his political ties to gain access to government databases for his own private purpose, claiming he wanted to conduct a background search to learn more about a woman he fancied, but wasn't exactly sure about. No one would dream of questioning such a harmless request from someone so renowned for his honesty. The chance to help him out in his personal life was looked upon as an honour. Many foresaw him leading the country one day. And while lying and putting his reputation on the line had caused the young politician no small amount of anxiety, he'd felt compelled in his heart of hearts to do whatever it took to make things right. In this case, he had convinced himself that the end justified the means.

The plan had paid off. He was able to locate our young man. The most recent records, dated some months ago, indicated that he'd been enrolled at an institution of higher learning located no great distance away. Surely nothing drastic had changed in so short a timeframe. Eager to confront his demons face-to-face, the young politician had left without a moment's delay.

Upon arrival at the campus where our young man was studying, the young politician had wasted no time surveying the school's grounds in determined hopes of catching sight of the grown-up version of the boy he'd bullied. He would finally make amends with both other and self. Hours passed to no avail.

Just as the young politician was about to throw in the towel and brand himself an imbecile for having made the journey, he'd spotted an individual he felt certain was his man walking alongside two others he had never seen before. A rush of nervousness ran through him. He took in a deep breath before setting foot in their direction.

While pacing across the lawn to interrupt the trio and request a moment's privacy with our young man, the young politician had received an inopportune call from a lobbyist of great consequence. The timing could not have been worse. He'd had no choice but to answer and find somewhere private to talk. He'd already taken a big risk with the unscheduled and unexplained absence. Having confirmed with his own eyes that our young man was, in fact, present at the school, he'd reasoned that it wouldn't be difficult to find him again. Besides, our young man might be alone next time, which would make things less awkward for and easier on everyone. Satisfied that the path to inner peace was within reach, the young politician, after pausing with a sad smile at his long-ago classmate, had hurried off to find a quiet nook to take his call.

As it turned out, the young politician had witnessed the very moment the direction of our young man's life would change forever. It was the next day that he would be apprehended by the authorities. By taking a future event for granted, the young politician had missed his chance.

The young politician had spent the entire next day searching for our young man, but all roads led to the same, exasperating nowhere. He couldn't file a formal inquiry with the school's administration for fear of being recognized as a public official and raising any suspicions about what it was he was doing and who it was he was looking for. Nobody he'd asked informally either recognized or had heard of our young man. The young politician was at a loss. Perhaps, he'd rationalized, this was a sign that the matter was best left alone. Nonsense! He wasn't one to give up so easily. He would try again the next day.

Tomorrow, in this case, had proved to be the bearer of bad news. News sites everywhere had broadcast our young man's name for his arrest in connection with *The Great Awakening*. Stunned by what he'd been reading, the young politician couldn't believe his bad luck.

Naturally, he'd followed the story with great interest. What had perplexed him most was that, in a matter of months, our young man had gone from freshman to dropout to high-profile criminal suspect. What had changed? Moreover, how was it that our young man was the only person the authorities had apprehended? Knowing firsthand the level of sophistication and resources required to carry out campaigns on such a large scale, the young politician had surmised how many others must have been involved and found it surprising that the authorities had remained clueless as to who any of them were.

The two associates the young politician had seen walking with our young man the day before had leapt to mind as leads to pursue. Perhaps they could help.

What had begun as a pilgrimage to find solace was fast becoming a secret obsession and personal investigation. With a healthy serving of new intrigue added to the mix, the young politician had decided to track down the mystery duo to ask them a few questions.

The next morning, with nothing more to go on than the location where he'd first observed them, the young politician had retraced his steps and waited anxiously. His persistence had quickly paid off; he'd spotted one of our young man's two associates—the Activist—walking hurriedly beneath the foliage of a row of trees, books in hand. Determined not to let a second opportunity slip away, the young politician had broken into a jog toward them.

The Activist, of course, had had no way of knowing that the intentions of the stranger running in their direction were harmless. For all the Activist knew, the law was closing in after our young man's capture. Unwilling to trust a soul outside of their close circle of trust, the Activist had ditched their books and took flight.

A dramatic pursuit by foot had ensued, causing many an onlooker to crane their rubbernecks and many an innocent bystander to yelp before jumping out of harm's way. The young politician had called out reassurances that he meant no harm, but there wasn't a guarantee in the world that could have convinced the highly distrustful and paranoid Activist. The chase was on.

After some distance, the young politician turned on the jests and pinned the squirming Activist into submission. Huffing and puffing, but no longer struggling after coming to terms with the fact that it was of no use, the Activist had made clear that under no circumstances would anything be divulged. In response, the young politician had explained who he was and how the two of them had come to be where they then found themselves. Calming down by degrees, the Activist had begun to slowly and cautiously trust that the young politician wasn't a threat, and could possibly even be of great assistance.

Over the course of their increasingly civilized exchange, a foundation of trust and openness had been established. The young politician had even let the Activist in on a plan he'd been up all night devising to help our young man escape prison. If it were to succeed, he would need the Activist's sworn allegiance, total confidence, and full cooperation. The Activist had been all ears.

A new alliance began forming between two individuals who, although seemingly incompatible on the surface, had a shared interest. Each had understood that they could profit or be undone by the other. Thusly, a tacit compact between the two otherwise mismatched parties had been forged. Symbiosis of purpose has the strangest tendency to bring together the most peculiar pairings.

The young politician then explained to our young man how they carried out his escape. To evade detection, they had taken every conceivable precautionary measure. This meant that as few people as were necessary to the plan's flawless execution were let in on it. Both the young politician and the Activist had become experienced at keeping secrets under lock and key, so that wouldn't be an issue.

The young politician had then assembled a small team of confidants to help execute the mission. In addition to the Activist, there was the great and revered indigenous chief. A political ally of the young politician's, the chief could provide a safe haven for our young man in his sovereign nation, out of the jurisdiction and, therefore, the reach of mainstream authorities. Investigators had already come around on a few occasions to make inquiries in the weeks following the escape, but they had been sent away in the same way they would have for nosey probes of any other nature.

Next, there was an ardent and enthusiastic volunteer the young politician had met on the campaign trail, an ardent follower of the young politician and his unifying philosophy. A prison guard by profession, he had believed in the young politician's message implicitly. Any time the two had happened to cross paths, he would go out of his way to offer the young politician his unconditional support. *Whatever the young politician needed*, the prison guard would stress.

No stranger to such declarations of unconditional loyalty and offers of help from his more fervent supporters, the young politician had taken note, filed it away, and thought no more of it. It wasn't until the young politician had discovered the need for a prison insider that he summoned the recollection and consulted the database of his campaign trail volunteers.

After spending a painstakingly long time sifting through the registry of names and cross-referencing their corresponding professions, he'd eventually pinpointed his man. In a divine stoke of happenstance, the devoted volunteer worked at the very high-security prison holding our young man captive.

A few nights later, the young politician, dressed incognito and hiding in a laneway free of cameras, had intercepted the prison guard on his way home from work. Quickly revealing his identity to prevent a scene, the young politician confided that he needed the prison guard's help freeing a political prisoner. The prison guard had accepted without hesitation or condition. The young politician had his word. They had found their inside man.

The young politician noted to our young man that all present in the room knew the devastating outcome of the prison guard's involvement. In his feverish bid to exorcise the unrelenting torment of guilt, the young politician had placed yet another innocent life in harm's way, this time resulting in a wholly unnecessary death. The burden on his tortured conscience had doubled. He could never forgive himself. But that was his cross to bear.

The young politician regained his composure before resuming. Lastly, there was the getaway driver, a relative of the chief who had regular work delivering goods to and from the reserve. The plan had required a failsafe means of transporting our young man after his escape, and in this driver they had just that. They'd planned the escape so that it corresponded precisely with the timing and direction of one of the getaway driver's regular late-night routes.

Our young man stopped the young politician there. What did he mean *lastly*? There had only been four of them? Why hadn't anyone mentioned a single word about the most important person of all? Why were they being so evasive? What were they hiding from him? She *was* okay, wasn't she?

After exchanging glances with the young politician and the chief, the Activist, speaking with both lowered voice and gaze, regretted to inform our young man that they had some difficult news to relay.

Paralyzed with fear at the thought that our young woman had found someone new and moved on, our young man braced himself for the worst.

Visibly uncomfortable with having to play messenger, the Activist didn't mince words in explaining that our young lady had developed the same aggressive cancer as her identical twin. She had been predictably stoic in the face of her chronic and deadly disease, but people didn't succumb to cancer because they lacked strength or courage; certain cancers were simply unbeatable, and this was one of them.

Stunned by the profound reality and finality of what he had just been told, our young man experienced what can only be described as instant and all-consuming anguish. The blood drained from his face and he covered his mouth to stop himself from being sick. The love of his life, the centre of his universe, was dead.

The room fell silent. Without making any attempt at offering empty words of comfort, the Activist handed our young man a piece of folded up paper. Holding back a torrent of tears, our young man unfurled the page to discover that it was a note our young lady had written to him from her deathbed. His lips quivered at the sight of her handwriting.

She loved him first and foremost, and her love would endure eternal with unabating constancy as she made the transition from this to the next life, whatsoever that final journey might entail. As she wrote, she could hear the angels' voices beckoning. It was the winter of her brief time on earth, and what a time it had been. She thanked him for believing in her and inspiring her to follow her heart and dreams. They had done what they said they would do—lay it all on the line in defense of tomorrow. Without him, she would not have had the strength to carry on, let alone make manifest such lofty ambitions. With her time near at hand, it was now his responsibility to take up the mantle and lead the popular uprising the rebels had ignited. The task was titanic, and the road perilous, but if anyone were equal to it, it was he. His capture and subsequent rise to fame was no accident. She had sensed that there was something special about him from the first. It was more than just his looks and charm that had caused her to fall for him. Wink. His imprisonment had caused her to temporarily second-guess her prophecy, but her eventual introduction to the young politician and his plan had restored her faith in full. She had initially intended to share everything with him, but ultimately decided against it to avoid the potential for any slip-ups. Please accept her apologies for keeping her illness and impending death from him. She was all too aware that she'd been the only thing keeping him going while he was locked away. She missed him dearly. If only she could have a few more months so she could see him, smell him, touch his face one last time. The pain caused by their separation far outweighed that of the cancer. By the time he was free and read this letter, however, she would be gone—forever. That was the harsh reality of a life that never promised to be fair. But wasn't it true that it was better to have loved and lost? The answer for her was a resounding *yes*. The clock was fast approaching midnight on her life. Her sister and his mother awaited her on the other side. She'd be sure to give them both his best. Take courage, brave soul. It was now in his hands. Love, Signed.

Upon completing his reading of the letter, our young man, feeling the tremendous weight it is possible for a single sheet of paper to contain, allowed it to slide through his fingertips and onto the floor. The Activist then added that, as she drew her final breath, our young woman, with a volume of voice no more audible than a gentle breeze playing upon a cluster of reeds, repeated her undying love for him. Those had been her final words.

After a moment's silent reflection, our young man wiped the streaming tears from his cheeks and swallowed back a wave of emotional outpouring. His visitors watched as he resumed sifting through the final pages contained in the folder.

In the days following the publication of the open letter penned under our young man's name, exhorting the purchase of land, the deluge of donations to the International Conservation Cooperative (ICC) surpassed anything anyone could have foreseen as being possible. Totaling in the billions after the first seventy-two hours alone, sums big and small had started pouring in from rich and poor alike. Whether people truly believed in the movement, didn't want to be left out of something most everyone else seemed to be taking part in, or simply contributed to see how far this thing could go, people from all walks of life had given freely and generously. Media outlets couldn't churn out new content fast enough to meet the demand of readers. Street interviews of random passersby had provided proof that it was all anyone could think about. Seeing the opportunity to capitalize, landowners and corporations had made haste to put their properties on the market at vastly inflated prices; the prospect of a quick profit had been irresistible. Governments had scrambled to block sales where possible, but, by and large, unprotected land had sold like hotcakes. Some governments had even taken the controversial step of putting lands that were earmarked for various development projects on the market to capitalize on the irresistibly high returns. The combined purchase power of the people had started to flex its seemingly unlimited muscle. Unlike tax dollars, however, the enormity of its collective strength wouldn't be undercut by bloated bureaucratic red tape. On a scale unrivaled in the annals of history, this had been the purest, most widespread and powerful example of governance for and by the people the world had ever known. Oddly enough, it blended two extreme and opposing ideological foes: communism and libertarianism.

With that, the contents of the folder compiled for the purpose of helping our young man fill the gaping gap in his memory came to a close. After having spent multiple weeks in a vegetative state, he had recovered to learn that, during the bottomless depths of his comatose slumber, his name had been used to galvanize people numbering in the scores of millions to join financial forces in the name of leaving a habitable planet to their offspring, a concept the ancestors of the great chief had passed on to their young for millennia.

The Activist begged our young man's forgiveness for having used his identity for the open letter without his permission. Since the time of the escape, his health had been in a grim state, to put it mildly. It didn't look like he would survive, so they had decided to leverage his name while it was still fresh and influential in people's minds. None would be any the wiser that he was on death's doorstep. If a miracle happened and he was restored to full health, the consensus was that he would understand. The Activist hoped he understood. Did he?

Looking away, our young man nodded in the affirmative.

The Activist went on to explain that, one day, as she lay on her deathbed, our young lady had begun to explain the concept of an international conservation cooperative out of the blue. Crediting our young man with the idea, she'd requested, as her dying wish, that the Activist and the young politician leverage the momentum of *The Great Awakening* to make his vision a reality. They had the critical mass of support they needed. All they had to do was invoke our young man's name once they freed him from prison. She had believed beyond dissuasion that *he* was the chosen one, destined to change the course of history, and could not, under any circumstances, be convinced to the contrary.

Feeling that these grandiose proclamations stemmed more from her delirious state and failing condition than anything else, the Activist had felt compelled to promise they would do everything in their power. It was owed to her for all she had done for the cause. Besides, there was undeniable merit to the idea. They had already garnered the widespread public attention and support they'd need for the concept of an international cooperative to really catch on. It might just be crazy enough to work. The young politician and the chief had agreed.

Adding to her prophetic legend, our young lady's foretelling had come true exactly as predicted. The open letter the three associates had ghostwritten using our young man as their *nom de plume* had worked to great effect. With our young man's mythical reputation and the fear induced by a natural disaster of biblical proportions still fresh in their minds, the public had glommed onto the ICC as if it were a lifeboat after a shipwreck.

Then, in a most welcome twist of good fortune, our young man had unexpectedly rebounded from months of what looked to be the slow encroachment of death. And thus they found themselves here today, in a nondescript little room on a remote indigenous reservation.

Overwhelmed by the gravity of everything he had just learned, our young man, with swelling setting in around his grief-stricken eyes, requested a moment to digest it all. Lacking the energy to react outwardly, he remained transfixed in a state of dazed astonishment. How could he ever live up to the impossibly high expectations his love and his three associates had set for him? He could barely stand up of his own accord let alone carry the weight of the world on his shoulders. They'd have had a better chance of success had he done them all a favour and died. Dead men no longer betray their mortal shortcomings; flaws and insecurities get buried alongside them. What a relief death would be from his insufferable emotional and physical pain. His heart wasn't just broken; it had disintegrated into a mound of ash.

But this was no time for grief, and it certainly wasn't time to feel sorry for himself. That wasn't what she'd wanted. She had wanted him to rise to the occasion. He owed it to her to cast aside his petty insecurities, face his fears, and give it his best try. Her memory impelled him. Her words emboldened him. He may not have been deserving of his newfound celebrity, but the spotlight was on him whether he liked it or not. If ever there was an opportunity to prove his worth, it was then. *Carpe diem.*

With that, our young man dedicated himself mind and body to the restoration of robust health. He unleashed a voracious appetite, devouring food at a rate faster than his host nation could prepare it. Having learned while in prison that Nelson Mandela would jog on the spot for a considerable amount of time each day while on the lam, our young man, the moment his legs could support him, did just that each morning before sunrise. He planned, thought, wrote, and discussed from dawn to sundown. As his strength returned, with it came a sense of courage he had never known himself to have. He was discovering that resilience is the ability to get back up after we've been knocked down, and our young man bounced back stronger than ever. Something different, something peerless and inimitable, had been activated inside him. His height hadn't changed, but he stood as a giant amongst men.

Meanwhile, public support continued to climb and money continued to pour in. A legal team composed of sympathizers was assembled through the young politician's close circle of influence to facilitate the purchase of land on behalf of the ICC without betraying the identities or whereabouts of its leaders. All was protected by the law as privileged and confidential.

Acres numbering in the millions were being purchased through the combined wealth of millions for the purpose of being kept off-limits from developers in perpetuity. Wills were amended so that individuals' transfers of wealth would continue to contribute to the ICC upon death. Landowners, corporations, and, in many cases, governments were getting rich in the process. Many who had initially scoffed at the idea eventually succumbed to the hysteria and reached for their wallets. In true human fashion, monkey saw, monkey did, and it was all in the name of preserving trees.

An unprecedented international revolution was unfolding in real time, and a resultant sense of togetherness between complete strangers spanning the spectrum of walks of life was being established. Literal common ground was bridging longstanding chasms created by superficial differences. Utopian ideals such as world peace no longer felt like a pipe dream. Never had such optimism swept the globe. By the increasingly agnostic standards of the day, our young man had become more famous than Jesus, Mohammed, and Buddha combined. The winds of change were gathering speed.

XV

After a series of behind-the-scenes emergency meetings between global tycoons and influential leaders from the general assembly of nations, a decision was reached to hurriedly pass a newly recommended resolution into international law. A minority of moderate voices opposed the extreme measures as anti-democratic, but they were drowned out by those who hadn't any choice but to back it. Most leaders were at the mercy of their powerful donor base. It so happened that a lot of really rich people had gotten really rich destroying the planet. The ICC spelled big trouble for their never-ending expansion plans.

The newly introduced international law was defined along the following lines:

> *A conspiracy between individuals and/or institutions and/or nations to deny the use of land for the purpose of economic development and, consequently, the betterment and prosperity of human civilization shall be considered no different and treated no differently than the abduction or taking hostage of a person or persons by a terrorist cell or organization, thereby placing any participating party on equal footing with and subjecting them to the same severe consequences as terrorists.*

Governments then deployed their poison-tongued spin-doctors to launch a far-reaching public relations campaign aimed at gently scaring people into abandoning the ICC. The persuaders-cum-brainwashers sounded dire warnings that our young man's propaganda was the hypnotizing dog whistle of a conniving, manipulative, and power-thirsty occult leader who managed to dupe a fraction of the world into following him, much as the Pied Piper lured rats and children in the mystical realms of yore. The rising environmental threat facing humanity was real, they acknowledged, and the fact that humans were a primary contributing factor was well documented and indisputable. This was all truth. The path to reversing the damage, however, would not be determined by agitators stirring up anarchy in absence of the sober application of bureaucratic and scientific due diligence. There were rules. There were processes. There was a pecking order that was to be respected and adhered to. The sky had its fair share of problems, granted, but it was in no way falling. A true, sustainable solution would instead be brought about by policy development based on the latest highly credible, evidence-based information without jeopardizing prosperity in the process. That was the established and, therefore, right way to get things done.

Scientific innovation had advanced leaps and bounds in the last few years alone, they continued, using language a cobra couldn't resist dancing to. White lab coats and business suits with briefcases were on the verge of great things. The establishment's brightest minds were working around the clock to convert your hard-earned money into a better tomorrow. And the promise of jobs, jobs, jobs on top of it all! Growth without end was on the line here. Think of how great your life could be! Why make sacrifices when you've the promise of gains? They were the ones to side with.

Like curing cancer, the spin doctors' most recent appeal was, like all previous appeals, presented as being the one just around the corner from the breakthrough we've all been waiting for.

It was understandable that people were still shaken from and grieving the great flood, continued the propaganda machine, but overreacting by destabilizing society was not the answer. What was needed was healing and rebuilding—and faith—not the abandonment of law and order. How very insulting to the victims of the great flood. If anyone needed citizens' combined resources, it was the victims. What about the victims?

Unlike our fugitive young man's harebrained scheme, governments had the people's best interests at heart in all they did, as they always had and forever would. That's why they had been elected fair and square, no? Did it make sense to call into question time-tested and sacred democratic institutions at a time when they were needed most? If things truly were so calamitous and dire, was it wise to gamble on what amounted to no more than a thinly veiled plot by an egocentric narcissist to stir up mayhem and make a name for himself? The answer, on the remote possibility it, for some reason, wasn't already clear, was a resounding *no*. His fifteen minutes of fame were up.

Governments domestic and foreign announced they would be joining forces with financial institutions to freeze all monies invested for the intended purpose of participating in an international conspiracy to commit largescale economic terrorism. Like money laundering and other financial crimes, tolerance for the movement of illicit funds would be zero. Clemency and reimbursement would be granted to those who voluntarily came forward and paid a small fine within a given timeframe. Governments weren't monsters; they understood that it was easy to get swept up in the fever of a mob mentality. They were willing to forgive at a small price so long as people were willing to own up to the error of their ways.

The choice, they made clear, was that or harsh punishment and a criminal record. Those who chose to remain rogue would be subjected to the swift and full force of the law. It was up to them; this was their non-negotiable ultimatum. Be good and repent. Everything will be fine and go back to normal provided they do the right thing and atone.

Understandably, many people lost their nerve and withdrew their support of the Cooperative out of self-preservation. Fear forced their hands to seek forgiveness for their supposed sins and to have their good names stricken from the outlaw ledger. They didn't have to be told twice. Doing so was no indication of weakness, either. They were primates like the rest of us, doing what was necessary to survive in the civilized wild. How could they be blamed? *Flight.*

But surprisingly, a rather significant proportion of people didn't budge. Knowing so many others shared in their conviction manifested itself as collective bravery. Never had human beings tapped so deeply into the power of numbers. All felt they were nodes connected to an energy grid far greater than themselves. Abandoning the ICC meant abandoning their fellow man, uprooting themselves from the fertile soils of a thick and indestructible forest. A long searched for, profound sense of meaning and universal kinship had been unearthed. Outweighing their fear of reprisal, this newfound sense of shared empowerment wasn't something any in this latter camp were willing to give up so easily. Confident in the might of their unified front, they quite literally stood their ground. *Fight.*

Spontaneous demonstrations began surfacing in municipalities big and small. In most cases, they were peaceful in nature, but in others, they became aggressive and riotous; picketing and the indiscriminate destruction of property stood at opposite ends of this spectrum. Windows were smashed in. Vehicles were overturned and set ablaze. Looting and random assaults were reported. Uneasiness gripped the domestic and international consciousness, with many sensing that life as they knew it was about to give way to the Unknown.

With panic and disorder mounting, governments had the just cause they needed to invoke martial law—the rioting and destruction had delivered it right into to their laps. They accused the terrorists of fomenting social unrest, vowing to track down every one of the agitators until peace and safety were returned to daily life. Boots met rib cages; bayonets met cheekbones; Tasers met the sides of necks; tear gas met eyes and choked lungs; and, in cases where it was argued to have been warranted, bullets pierced skulls, lodging themselves into brains. Row upon row of disciplined and well-coordinated police officers clad in riot gear marched behind an ominous wall of impregnable shields. Defenseless protesters were toppled. Examples had to be made of these thugs to discourage others who might consider following their lead. In the process, the gavel of the law also crushed defenseless citizens for peacefully standing up for what they believed in. The ever-ambiguous line between justice and injustice became even more blurred.

And what of the agitators' fearless leader? asked government spokespeople. What kind of bravery was it to hide in the shadows whilst the blood of so many flowed into sewer grates in his cowardly name? Real men—real leaders—walked the talk; they led the charge. So, where was *he*? If he really believed in his extremist cause and cared for those writhing in the gutters, he would step forward and call the people off before things got even more out of hand. This was not a battle he had any hope of winning. Good, from the authorities' perspective, always triumphed over evil. Order would be restored by any means necessary. It was a matter of time. He had it in his power to prevent further bloodshed. Do the right thing. Surrender and talk it out.

Buoyed by an ocean of public support, our young man emerged from his rehabilitation with redoubled energy and determination. He knew what had to be done. The authorities were right about one thing; it was time to finally show his face. Peaceful demonstrations had turned violent, and his name was at the centre of it all. People were dying in the streets. His was the only voice the rioting masses would listen to. It was his duty to intervene. And so, against the protestations and cautions put forth by his three associates who felt he wasn't yet ready, our young revolutionary requested that they film him addressing the state of affairs gripping the world.

In the video, he urged restraint, peace, and calm above all else. If the ICC were to have any chance of succeeding, it had to be through non-violent, lawful means. Violence only served to undermine the legitimacy of their cause. Whether or not they felt the decisions of governments to be just, lawlessness did them no favours. Their strength wasn't in disparate acts of individual vandalism and violence. Anarchy was self-defeating. They mustn't give the authorities cause to demonize them any further. For this to work, restraint was essential. Their true power was in their ability to mobilize and coordinate peacefully on a global scale to remind governments who was serving whom. Power *to* the people; power *for* the people, and power *by* the people. Together, humans could force the established order to bend to their will without so much as breaking a law or a smile. Together, and only together, could they safeguard Mother Nature for future generations. The bell had tolled. The time to stand together in a universal show of human solidarity was upon them.

He then designated a day and time for people from all nations to march, cycle, train, wheel, boat, drive electric vehicles, etc., to the doorsteps of their respective national governments for a worldwide protest on a scale heretofore unwitnessed. Every participant mattered. Each resistor made as critical and significant an impact as the next. The larger the crowds, the greater their sway. This was too important a moment to shrink away from. Together, they would not, could not, be denied.

For his part, our young man gave his word that he would attend the protest in his homeland, standing shoulder-to-shoulder with his fellow man, woman, and child on the front lines. There, from the main amphitheatre in his nation's capital, he would address the world. The authorities were welcome to capture and detain him, but doing so would be considered a direct violation of the people's will. Silence him if they dared.

United, organized, and self-restrained, the human species would set aside its superficial differences and join forces as a united front in defense of its children, their children, and their children after them. They would take back the planet and implement the necessary measures to protect it from further catastrophic harm.

Shortly after the video was anonymously leaked to the press, it went completely viral. It seemed everyone knew about it. As if a spell had suddenly been cast over the land, the widespread vandalism and violence came to an abrupt halt. People, with astonishingly few exceptions, abandoned their hooliganism and resumed the law-abiding lives they had put on hold as if nothing at all had happened. If not for the physical evidence, there'd have been no indication of the widespread turmoil that, mere hours earlier, had been in full swing in dozens of countries. Although things returned to normal on the surface, an eerie silence pervaded the air. It was as if the entire planet were holding its breath.

While the authorities rounded up and made an example of criminals caught red-handed on closed circuit surveillance, social media posts, and other such ubiquitous means of recording all that took place in public life, the young politician explained to the inner circle that a good turnout at the planned international protest was in no way a sure thing. Numerous polls suggested that fence-sitters—the majority of respondents—were still deliberating the wisdom in taking part. Although the average citizen reportedly supported the movement in their heart of hearts, the thought of risking everything gave them serious pause and cause for reconsideration. These individuals were aware of the magnitude of what was at stake in the grand scheme, but they were also perfectly content with their lives and liberties just the way they were. Why ruin a good thing for an uncertain outcome, even if it felt like the right thing to do? Did they really want to be associated with a high-profile fugitive and potentially charged as criminals? They had watched clip after clip of examples being made of the rioters. Was putting it all on the line—comfort, happiness, the whole of it—worth it?

XVI

In the days leading up to the international protest, time, ever the great revealer, began to pull back the curtains on how successful the recruitment efforts of our young revolutionary had been. What unfolded far exceeded what anyone would have thought possible in their wildest imagination. Mass human migration events began taking shape in countries on every continent. Like wildebeest and zebras crossing the African plains or caribou traversing North America, herds of Homo sapiens stretching as far as the naked eye could see made their way to their respective nations' capitals. Automotive traffic on major highways came to a standstill as hundreds of thousands of walkers and cyclists equipped with provisions to last weeks travelled in unison along major arteries. People with disabilities burned through several pairs of gloves wheeling themselves. Packed trains left station platforms at regular intervals.

An international protest unparalleled in the pages of history textbooks was taking shape.

As the migrants passed through villages, towns, and cities, opponents gathered in large crowds to hurl insults and objects at them, doing their best to antagonize and fan the flames of confrontation. But they were no match for the enormity of the travelling caravans. Reminding themselves of our young revolutionary's call for peace and lawfulness under any circumstance, the migrant protesters exercised Zen-like self-restraint in the face of adversity. The moment it looked like someone might lose his cool or her nerve, others nearby, most times perfect strangers, would intervene and ensure cooler heads prevailed. In all the bags, luggage, and provisions being transported all those kilometers and miles, not a solitary ego had been packed. As advertised, the Cooperative triggered widespread cooperation.

People who weren't participating were following the event with rapt attention. Time came to a standstill. The economy—nay—society was put on hold. Human beings found themselves in uncharted territory. No one knew what to expect.

In response to this massive mobilization of human beings, security presence was beefed up where possible, but the magnitude of the migrations dwarfed the resource capabilities of many jurisdictions. Intervention by force was simply out of the question without clear and defensible cause. Soldiers and police officers were under strict orders to refrain from the use of force unless it was out of absolute and obvious necessity. There were too many people and there was too much at stake.

Not since the great world wars had the coordinated mobilization of people on such an exceptionally large scale taken place. On this occasion, however, those marching were unarmed. On this occasion, all wore the same uniform—human skin.

During the middle of the night prior to the morning he was to be transported to the protest in his home country, our young revolutionary leader awoke out of breath and in a cold sweat. Disoriented and unsure of the time, he could sense that he was not alone in the room in which he had been lodging since his escape. Before his eyes could adapt to the darkness around him, he could make out what looked to be a dark curtain swaying in the breeze by the window. Only, there were no curtains in the room. A chill ran down his spine.

He called out to the apparition but received no reply. After rubbing his eyes to make sure they weren't playing tricks on him, they assured him that the haunting figure remained, testing the limits of his nerve. He sat up in his bed and leaned forward to inspect the matter more closely. What he saw caused him to gasp with fright.

Rising to his feet, our young revolutionary crept slowly and cautiously toward the ghoulish figure. As he drew nearer, the presence came clearer into view. Upon realizing who it was, the blood drained from his face and his hands went numb. He was staring up at his own, lifeless corpse dangling from the ceiling.

In a panic-stricken reflex, he stumbled backward and lunged for the light switch on the wall. The initial shock of brightness made him squint. As his sight adjusted, he let out a sigh of relief. The specter had vanished.

Reasoning that he must have been in that intermediate realm that straddles the conscious and subconscious mind, our young revolutionary regained his composure by degrees. Sunrise would mark the dawn of the biggest day of his life. He needed sleep. Returning to his bed, he soon sank back into the deepest of slumbers this side of death.

XVII

The day of the protest had arrived. Media coverage portrayed vast seas of protesters gathering in the great squares of great capital cities around the world. In some cases, it was early morning. In others, it was the middle of the night. The only incidents to report were of the odd protester collapsing from exhaustion or panicking due to claustrophobia. Otherwise, all was civil in the early goings. To describe the crowd sizes as "large" fell significantly short of the mark, but hyperbole didn't quite do them justice either. There were no words.

Those who didn't participate directly watched on in utter amazement at what they were witnessing. If they weren't there in person, their eyes were glued to some form of screen, virtually teleporting themselves from the safety of their own homes and places of work. Commerce paused; receding global markets, having experienced extreme volatility since the great flood, remained on pins and needles in anxious anticipation of how things would unfold. Parents kept their children close for fear that all hell might break loose. The unknown weighed heavily. The past contained no wisdom to call upon.

To evade the notice of authority, our young revolutionary was smuggled to the protest by a First Nations convoy. As he lay in a secret compartment hidden beneath the vehicle's flooring, he couldn't help but think of those who had travelled the Underground Railroad in harrowing attempts to flee the horrors of the human slave trade. That had been an extreme example of humanity at its worst, reducing its fellow man to the status of brute. But who were the real brutes? When we invalidated the dignity of others, we, in turn, forfeited our own. We were all of us brutes.

The site of the protest in the capital city of our young revolutionary's home country could only be described as an indescribable assembly of people. Outside of the main square, where air had difficulty maneuvering in the dense crowd, the streets were clogged with individuals of all shapes, abilities, sizes, and colours spanning multiple concentric city blocks. Aside from designated emergency laneways, driving a vehicle through the crowd was out of the question. Late arrivals were forced to park some distance away and walk until they met the expanding outer reaches of the swelling crowds. It wasn't much easier for bicyclists, of which there was no shortage. Aerial views captured the enormity of the spectacle. Human beings bunched together in a show of unprecedented solidarity, stretching as far the reddening horizon and beyond. It was a security nightmare. All it would take was a single spark to set the entire matchbox ablaze.

That our young revolutionary had the power to trigger a riot of apocalyptic proportions was not lost on the authorities. The young politician had received insider information that highly coordinated, undercover military personnel were strategically positioned throughout the city. They had been given strict orders to spot and intercept our young revolutionary once the opportunity to do so swiftly and discreetly presented itself. The command from on high was to take all necessary measures to prevent the insurgent fugitive from reaching the main amphitheatre where he planned to speak. They would stop him before he ever got the chance. Once they apprehended him, the plan was to make it look like he was welcome to speak, but was ultimately too cowardly to show his face and make good on his word. That way, the authorities could easily manipulate popular sentiment back in their favour without risking unthinkable consequences. He had been offered a chance to appeal to the masses in person but had wound up retreating with his tail firmly tucked between his legs. He was nothing more than a self-serving dissenter full of hot air and empty promises. Not a word would be heard from him again. Theories would magically surface in the press claiming that he withdrew to a life of obscure exile before committing suicide. From there, trust in and subservience to governments and the established order could finally be restored to their proper place. Society would slowly pick up the pieces and life would return to normal. For it to work, his timely and discreet capture was not an option. The orders were given in no uncertain terms.

This meant that getting our young revolutionary to the main square to address the world would be a practically impossible mission. He was considered Public Enemy Number 1. How would he possibly reach such a public and heavily scrutinized stage with a highly sophisticated network of intelligence lying in wait to inconspicuously remove him from the equation? If our young revolutionary were to reach his podium, a clever ruse would be needed.

Thankfully, the young politician was a politician, deft at pulling strings and gifted at the art of deception, even if neither were his preferred modus operandi. He would resort to one of the oldest tricks in the voluminous book of trickery: bait and switch.

The plan went as follows:

The young politician called an emergency meeting to inform his fellow elected officials that First Nations leaders— stakeholders who fell within his mandate, but were also secretly his trusted allies—had unexpectedly expressed their intention to speak out against the ICC in person at the protest. It was their belief that the Cooperative was far too radical in its approach. After countless generations spent protesting in extreme and counterproductive ways to no avail, the current assembly of chiefs had decided that enough was enough—anti-government, disruptive protests just weren't the way forward. It pained them to think of how much time had been lost that could have otherwise been spent working *alongside* governments to bring about mutually beneficial solutions. The Cooperative was, in effect, the antithesis of cooperation. It had taken them hundreds of years to finally come to terms with it, but the fact of the matter was that true cooperation involved consensus-building and compromise between everyone—governments and their constituents alike.

The young politician urged his political colleagues to permit the First Nations leaders to publicly state their case at the protest. He was willing to put his reputation on the line that it would work. Things were reaching a fever pitch and had the potential to become extremely dangerous. Public safety was under imminent threat. They were being offered an olive branch when they needed it most. First Nations leaders were volunteering to knock some much-needed sense into the brainwashed masses. In exchange for their support, all they sought in return was a formal contract agreeing to finally, after centuries of conflict and strife, recognize the full and absolute extent of First Nations sovereignty. It was the lesser of two evils by a long shot, a small price to pay to convert age-old adversaries into allies at a time when they needed them most. That was their offer, take it or leave it.

Desperate, the government, normally shrewd as criminal defense lawyers, was in no position to call anyone's bluff, especially one of their own. A small contingent voiced their apprehension, but a starving person will always choose to eat a meal that may or may not have been poisoned. The government was in a weakened position and, therefore, was susceptible to correspondingly weakened judgment. They signed the contract in good faith.

The chiefs, of course, had as much intention of honouring the contract as colonialists of the past had had of honouring theirs. Not only did they side unreservedly with the protesters, but there was no chance in hell they weren't taking full advantage of the best political leverage they had had since the early settlers first arrived and couldn't survive without them. It had been a long time coming.

Although the young politician risked his reputation and freedom for this grand political deception—and maybe even his life if ever he were to be tried and executed for treason— he would accept any consequence that came his way, including the ultimate sacrifice. He wouldn't rest until he'd atoned for the wrongs he had caused our young revolutionary and that young, innocent prison guard, rest his soul. Our young revolutionary must have his stage, if it was the last thing the young politician did. And so he put everything on the line to both make it happen for the benefit of mankind and to make things right with himself.

The bus concealing the man of the hour finally arrived at the outer perimeter of the protest in his home country. They were met at a designated point by military personnel tasked by government leaders with escorting the First Nations convoy to the main amphitheatre where they would make their appeal to the nation and the world.

As the caravan penetrated the crowd, our young revolutionary was filled with an incredible surge of nervous adrenaline. Anxious for a glimpse at his surroundings, he peeked through a small crack in the floor under which he hid. Through the top half of one of the vehicle's windows he could see the tops of city buildings juxtaposed against the sky. The sun was in the process of setting. The vibrations of energy radiating from without invigorated his being. Protesters standing near where the vehicle passed rapped on its sides and windows, shouting fleeting blurs of sound. It was dusk, but the gravity of his reality was dawning upon him. His podium awaited, and so, too, did an expectant world.

After several stops and starts, the procession finally came to a halt. A commotion of voices and shuffling above our young revolutionary's head indicated that the passengers beneath whom he had been stowed were gathering their belongings and preparing to disembark. The trap door was raised, and he was greeted by the outstretched arms of two enormous First Nations men. After being helped out of the hole, he was immediately covered in a traditional indigenous robe and headdress to conceal his identity. So draped was he in these oversized ceremonial vestments that he could barely see. Looking like a fabled shaman of old, our young revolutionary was no longer recognizable. His gargantuan bodyguards then ushered him off the bus and situated him at the rear of the line of First Nations delegates.

As he waited for his cue to proceed, our young revolutionary glanced over his shoulder at the endless crowd that had gathered at his request. The magnitude of it all caused his knees to momentarily weaken. To think, there were scores of protests just like this one taking place that very moment across the spectrum of geographies, cultures, and time zones. The pounding of his heart competed with the sound of the massive crowd. Like a native drum or Mother Nature's pulse, his body was kicking into gear, energizing and steadying him for his big moment. He was no longer acting entirely of his own accord. Something bigger, timeless, transcendent fueled him from within.

At the signal of a team of government officials who were tasked with welcoming the First Nations delegation, they were led though a heavily armed security barrier and up a set of stairs leading onto an empty stage under the glare of gigantic floodlights. The sun sank on the distant, crimson horizon. The moment stood before him. He stood before the moment.

As the First Nations leaders reached the top of the stairs, they parted to either side, carving out an opening through which our young revolutionary could be conveyed to the head of the pack. Pausing to gather himself before stepping fully into view, he was greeted by the young politician who matter-of-factly asked him if he was ready. In response, our young revolutionary gave a slight yet unmistakably confident nod in the affirmative. The young politician then placed a hand on his shoulder before wishing him good luck.

The stage was literally set. Like the inaugural moon landing, our young revolutionary took a small first step for himself; a giant leap for mankind. There was no turning back. As he emerged into view, cloaked in feathers and enshrouded in mystery, a hush came over the crowd. Who was this veiled figure standing before them? Wherever the conspiring government leaders were watching from, they were likely crossing their fingers in nervous anticipation, hopeful that their last-ditch plan would succeed. Suspense filled the air.

As his eyes adjusted to the blinding lights, our young revolutionary could make out the silhouette of a vast ocean of protesters eclipsing the blazing red skyline. As ready as he'd ever be, he shed himself of his disguise, exposing his identity for all to see. The moment they recognized the revolutionary figure on the screens situated in the capital square and elsewhere throughout the city, protesters who had travelled from far and wide greeted him with a thunderous roar, causing the stage to quake beneath his feet.

Recognizing their target was in plain sight without any risk of civilian casualties, strategically located sharpshooters and drones took aim. Military guards situated at stage level drew their weapons and began approaching the suspect with the intention of apprehending him. Before they could reach him, however, several unarmed First Nations men stood in their way, unflinchingly staring down the barrels of their high-powered weapons in a tense standoff. The authorities couldn't risk such a large-scale threat to public safety. They had been had, beaten at their own game by an insidious turncoat. Orders were given for snipers to hold their fire until further notice, and for the guards on stage to stand down. They had no choice but to let the fugitive address the crowd. The moment he exited the stage, they would detain him peaceably and quietly behind the scenes. All they could do for the moment was hold their breath. Guns were lowered. Hopefully, their most wanted man would figuratively shoot himself in the foot in the meantime.

Swallowing his fear, our young revolutionary approached the podium. All eyes were on him. After tapping the microphone to test whether it was on, he drew a final, fulsome breath of readiness and began.

As had been written in his open letter, human beings were at a turning point, a crossroads that would determine their fate as a species. Unlike old age, they weren't simply reaching the natural end of their species' lifecycle. In a multigenerational effort to leverage their evolutionary advantage over other species—the human brain—they had invested all their energies into manipulating the natural world to satisfy their insatiable thirst for power. At the root of it all was greed. The fulfillment of finite needs had long ago been distorted into the endless pursuit of infinite wants. Nothing was ever enough. Whole ecosystems were wiped out to feed the ill-conceived belief that economic growth was limitless, that natural resources were boundless. More than just willing to massacre all other forms of biota that sprang from Mother Nature's charitable bosom, human beings would unhesitatingly massacre their own in order to amass as much of the planet as they could for themselves.

Consequently, the planet's delicate balance had been upset, and the natural world—the fount required to sustain organic life—had been pushed to the brink of collapse. One had to look no further than the many symptoms of chronic disease for irrefutable proof: drought, pestilence, waste, disaster, extinction. And it was all happening at an accelerating rate. Mother Nature was gravely ill. The great flood was one in a succession of increasingly desperate bids by her immune system to rid her body of a deadly pathogen. As difficult as it was to come to terms with, that pathogen was the species Homo sapiens. The global scientific community was unanimous and had been for generations. Something had to give. Humans were left with a simple choice: reverse course or face the dire consequences.

Those attending the protests weren't there because of or to see *him*. Those who had voluntarily interrupted their personal lives to travel great distances and send a message to national governments in capitals around the world didn't actually care about *him*. He was just a symbol. They were there because they could no longer afford to ignore what was happening in plain sight. They were there based on a shared acknowledgement that swift and drastic measures were required to save their species, to save their planet, to save life.

The collective shirking of their God-given responsibility as stewards of the earth had gone on for too long. The buck had been passed down from generation to generation in the form of an heirloom dagger with which to stab tomorrow in the back. Our past was guilty of conspiring against our present. Our present was guilty of conspiring against our future. This was a long overdue global show of contrition. Father Time sat listening on the other side of the confessional, stroking his long, white beard as he considered what was being said.

There was no more room for denial, excuses, and procrastination. They were there to influence the elected officials and institutions that governed them and held sway over their daily lives into sweeping reforms. Power *to* the people; power *for* the people, and power *by* the people. There were enough of them now to dictate terms, and they knew it. The winds of change were gusting. A great and mighty revolution was sweeping the planet to preserve it for future generations.

At this, our young revolutionary paused and asked the measureless sea of likeminded protesters if they were with him. In response, they let out a mighty roar that would echo on so long as there were still ears to hear it. The same reaction took place simultaneously in capital cities the world over.

They had gathered on that fateful day, continued our young revolutionary, not only to show governments who was boss, but also to vow to atone for the damage they and their forefathers had caused. They must adopt whatever changes to their way of living were necessary to undo centuries of damage. They must also implement whatever measures were necessary to prevent future relapse. And so, as judge and jury—as well as defendant willing to come clean and own up to its actions— humans numerous enough to force the issue were prepared to charge, indict, and convict themselves of *crimes against posterity.* For their willingness to cooperate, and because the present inhabitants of the planet hadn't been the sole perpetrators of this intergenerational felony, their self-imposed sentence would be reduced to multiple lifetimes of community service consisting of everything within their power to restore Mother Nature to good health. If it meant making significant, life-altering sacrifices, so be it. Reparations had to be made. There would be no more second chances. They may not get to enjoy life's luxuries as much as they could have had they continued to turn a blind eye, but they would derive a far greater sense of fulfillment knowing they were the living population of human beings who swooped in at the eleventh hour to save the day and rescue tomorrow.

Our young revolutionary leader read their collective sentence, their repayment of debt to the whole of organic existence, along the following lines: In addition to the protection and restoration of vast swaths of land as agreed upon and funded by global citizens comprising the International Conservation Cooperative, individuals and corporations would be subject to substantial tax increases to fund a series of far-reaching, evidence-based conservation initiatives touching every aspect of daily life. Committees composed of the world's top climate change scientists, environmental economists, and other experts would be formed to direct policy and spending in all instances. If a proposed course of action didn't meet their approval, it didn't see the light of day. Subsidies and credits would be made available to incentivize and reward businesses and industries as they transitioned from unsustainable to sustainable models. The same went for individual households.

As for governments, they would be required to make available real-time accounting of tax revenue and spending to ensure nary a cent was misspent or misdirected for nefarious or bureaucratic purposes. The government was an apparatus built to serve the people, and so it would be bound to full transparency. The laws governing daily lives would undergo a complete overhaul to enforce universally sustainable decision-making. An international pact would be reached and an oversight body established.

Everything from manufacturing, packaging, and logistics to advertising and commerce would be reimagined and transformed. Transgressors would be penalized and adherents would be rewarded, accordingly. Strict limits would be imposed on consumerism; non-renewable energy would be phased out of existence; the production and consumption of meat would be closely monitored and strictly regulated on a per household basis, as would be human reproduction. The accumulation of waste would be punished harshly; the reuse or repurposing of resources would be rewarded in equal measure; a deadline would be set for a time when all plastics would be forbidden; funding for road repairs or other such deterioration-prone infrastructure projects would be diverted to more sustainable and economically bolstering projects like the installation of high-speed rail.

On and on our young revolutionary continued, sketching out the framework for a new world order in magnificently lucid detail.

Mass monoculture would be uprooted. Planned obsolescence would be rendered obsolete. If the magnates sitting atop the mountains of money they had amassed had a problem with this new world order, they could take it up with the everyday consumers who had already reclaimed their rightful sovereignty during *The Great Awakening*. The image of a slaveholder retreating from insurgent slaves was invoked. *We, the people.* Rail, solar, wind, geothermal, tidal, flora, fauna—planet earth had everything anyone could ever need and more, so long as it was properly harnessed, and humans resisted the temptation to take more than their fair share or to do so at a rate exceeding replacement. We were primates, after all, a bunch of monkeys that had strayed from the welcoming embrace of the forest and lost their way.

As our young revolutionary delivered his rousing speech, the crowd, hanging onto his every word as if it were holy scripture being delivered from the lips of a great prophet, cheered him on at the top of their voices any time he paused for effect or to catch his breath.

During one of these moments, he thought of how utterly remarkable it was that his life, so sad and unfortunate from the very start, had seen him rise to such unimaginable and improbable heights. He had defied the odds and more. If only his mother and our young lady could see him now. But somehow, some way, he knew they could. He could feel them, their presence, swirling about his being. The ghosts of history's great revolutionaries were there, too. As these thoughts swept across his fully activated mind, he resumed his speech with redoubled passion.

It was at the climactic height of this oratorical opus that a commotion in the crowd at the front of the stage caught his attention. Something about it, something familiar, sent an eerie feeling shooting down his spine. Was it déjà vu? Had he experienced this before? In a dream once, maybe?

He stepped away from the microphone momentarily to gather himself. Still preoccupied by a foreboding sensation, he returned to the podium and cleared his throat before resuming. He barely got a sentence out before the disturbance in the crowd intensified.

At that exact point in time, our young revolutionary experienced a sudden onset of intense weakness and disorientation. Had he been drugged? Dizzy, cold, and short of breath, he saw what appeared to be the outline of a figure at the foot of the stage holding a gun. And yet, he somehow felt as though he had already been shot multiple times. His reality became warped, as if he were somehow caught between two dimensions. The shrill scream of a terrified woman pierced through the tumult of the protesters. His conscious mind split in two and was in the process of recalibrating, like two experiences of the identical present converging into one. A wave of nervous energy rippled across the dark sea of people.

His immediate present was blending together with his immediate past, or was it the other way around? Time stood still. The intense light he had seen when he was beaten to within an inch of his life in grade school reappeared in his mind's eye, brilliant, vibrant, warm, and eternal. The beckoning voices of his mother and our young lady called to him from some faint and unknown distance. He strained for breath, but his lungs were flooded with his own blood. The figure at the foot of the stage took aim. His heart drummed its final beat. It was during that fateful, penultimate pause, that infinitesimally small sliver of time, that our young revolutionary heard the same loud bangs and saw the same bright flashes that he had seen just prior to the moment that his life flashed before his eyes.

Epilogue

The world is a stage, according to our friend William Shakespeare, and its inhabitants across the spectrum of genders (and species) are merely players. Once we've stepped out into the spotlight of that bright, life-giving orb above, there will be twists and turns, highs and lows, smiles and tears, comedy and tragedy, and an overarching quest for meaning and morality like with any good tale's plot. And while things mightn't turn out the way we expect them to or hope they will, all we can do is give it our best performance with the cards we've been dealt. For, even if we're born into a bit role of little significance in the grand scheme of it all, we're never without the potential to leave a positive and lasting impression on those around us, actors and audience alike. We don't have the power to cast ourselves, no, but through the development of our character, we can, over time, cast ourselves in a more powerful, meaningful, and lasting light. And so we mustn't fall into the trap of accepting our fate as insignificant, for any script can be revised; any chorus member can blossom and become a lead. As understudies, we must be prepared and willing at all times to step into the protagonist's gigantic shoes, strap on their shining armor, and draw their swords—now our own—in a duel to the death with a fire-breathing dragon in defense of everything that's good, for good must always prevail in the end.

We all—each of us—have the potential to be a hero in this life. Whether it's leading a revolutionary charge or simply being a good influence on our neighbours and our surrounding habitats, we can all do our part to make the world a better place. If at first the odds and chips seem to be stacked against us, we mustn't become discouraged and shrink away from adversity. In every trial, every obstacle, life is presenting us with a lesson, a test of our mettle from which, with a little admixture of determination, resilience, and, it must be admitted, good fortune, we can emerge stronger and wiser, and rise through the ranks from page to squire and, finally, knight. Should we die on the battlefield in defense of all that is noble and righteous, our legacy will be to pass on our courage—our legend—to our successors in the form of pure and inextinguishable inspiration. We shall teach our young the secret to removing Excalibur from the stubborn clutches of the stone so that they, too, can protect the sacred and enchanted forest from the ghastly forces of evil. We must act with honour and integrity so that others, our children, the ones who observe us at all times with impressionable awe and wonder, may follow our lead.

We must give it our best shot in this life, for, when it's all said and done, it could very well be all said and done. Death could conceivably be nothing more than inconceivable nothingness. As much as we pretend to and hope for a judicious and glorious eternity as a never-ending reward for a finite life well lived, none can be certain, despite the many superstitious claims to the contrary, that they know what lies backstage, on the other side of the red curtain separating life from death. As much as we want to believe in order to quell our undying mortal fear of death, there is no peeking. To truly get backstage, one must needs be *gone*. Until we cross that final threshold, we simply cannot know what awaits us; we're still living, and so we must live! As scary as it is to contemplate, we may never experience death, as death mightn't be an experience in the first place. And so, rather than living in anticipation of something that mightn't be, let us instead refocus that misplaced energy on existence itself. Because the only way for us to truly live on forever is by safeguarding a future for our descendants, by securing a tomorrow for our offspring.

And so, when we bring down the house for our grand finale, we must take great care and all possible pains to avoid leaving the stage of life in a state of disrepair or ruins. For there will be countless aspiring young thespians looking to follow our example, eager to one day take the lead in the age-old tale about the battle between life's two competing forces—good and evil.

When the curtain is finally called on our last act and we bow out of this life for the last time, let us do so with the knowledge that our children can pick up where we left off without the risk of the Globe Theatre collapsing around them. In the end, it is our solemn duty as stewards of this, our only planet, to ensure the continuation of ours and other species; the furtherance of *life*. Let us regain and maintain that balance.

The show must go on.

A champion of the humanitarian spirit, the author lives on the outskirts of Toronto, Canada, with his beloved family. There, when not succumbing to his ice hockey addiction, he takes great pleasure dabbling in all things creative.

Made in the USA
Columbia, SC
11 July 2021